THE
CELESTINA

THE

CELESTINA

A Novel in Dialogue

Translated from the Spanish by

LESLEY BYRD SIMPSON

UNIVERSITY OF CALIFORNIA PRESS
Berkeley, Los Angeles, London

University of California Press
Berkeley and Los Angeles, California

University of California Press, Ltd.
London, England

© 1955, 2006 by
The Regents of the University of California

ISBN 978-0-520-25011-6

Library of Congress Catalog Card No.: 55-7961

Printed in the United States of America
Designed by Rita Carroll

12   11   10   09   08   07   06
7   6   5   4   3   2   1

The paper used in this publication meets the minimum
requirements of ANSI/NISO Z39.48-1992 (R 1997)
(*Permanence of Paper*). ∞

PREFACE

The vast impact of *Don Quixote* on the thought and literature of the world has created the impression that it was the only great book ever to come out of Spain. The unaccountable dearth of translations from the Spanish certainly supports that legend, which was brought forcibly to my attention not long ago by one of my colleagues who demanded: "What *have* the Spaniards ever written besides *Don Quixote?*" It set me to thinking that perhaps scholars have been so preoccupied with treating the masterpieces of Spain as so many specimens to be examined under the microscope that they have ill served their many countrymen who like to read good books but who lack the time and the training to read them in the original—hence the notion that Cervantes was unique and that his genius blossomed in a desert. The truth is, of course, that that prince of gentle satirists came from a long line of writers remarkable for their learning and command of their incomparable language, as well as for their understanding of the springs of human action.

By common consent the greatest of Cervantes' literary forebears was the author of the *Tragi-Comedy of Calisto and Melibea*, more popularly known as *The Celestina*, first published, so far as we know, in 1499. In every respect *The Celestina* deserves a place alongside Cervantes' masterpiece, in originality, depth, handling of dialogue, and sure drawing of character. It is even superior to *Don Quixote* in its close-knit fabric and sustained tension. Its vitality is attested by the large number of Spanish editions: 80 by the end of the sixteenth century, 119 by 1952. Eighteen editions of the Italian translation appeared before 1551; fourteen French editions were published in that same century, while in England James Mabbe's translation, first published in 1631, was not reissued, to my knowledge, until 1894.

The neglect of *The Celestina* by the English reading public is, I think, not hard to account for. Mabbe's translation is, to be sure, written in inimitable Jacobean English, but his command of Spanish was far from perfect and his rendition suffers from many strange interpretations as a consequence. Moreover, he based his work upon the text of later "corrected" editions, which I shall discuss below. Mabbe's pages, besides, are burdened naturally enough with obsolete words, obscure subtleties, and outmoded syntax, which give his book a certain quaintness and antiquarian flavor, but which make it fatiguing for the reader of today.

Whatever the reason may be, we have lost contact with one of the unique creations of the human mind, written in the full flood of the Renaissance by a man who was saturated and delighted with humanistic learning, and tremendously excited by the discovery of Man. *The Celestina* is a veritable storehouse of popular speech, proverbs, folklore, and aphorisms, and, of course, is freighted with the classical allusions then in fashion; but the author somehow avoids the arid pedantry of many of his contemporaries. All his characters, to be sure, are given to sententious sayings, but they never step outside themselves, and the reader soon comes to accept this infinitely rich embroidery as completely right and precious.

The central plot of *The Celestina* is slight. Calisto, a humorless and half-mad egotist, tries to seduce Melibea, the lovely daughter of the noble Pleberio, into whose garden he has penetrated while hawking. He is made frantic by her rejection, which he takes as an intolerable affront to his "honor," for Calisto has more than a little of the eternal Don Juan about him. In his frustration he falls an easy prey to his scheming servant Sempronio who, in hypocrisy, double-dealing, casuistry, and garrulousness, is a not unworthy prototype of Iago. Sempronio solicits the aid of an ancient procuress, Celestina, "a witch, astute and wise in all evil things."

From the moment Celestina appears she dominates the story.

Her worldly wisdom, frankness, wit, learning, and deviousness; her superstition, vanity, and greed; her pagan delight in the pleasures of the flesh, and her sure-handed manipulation of her puppets, that is to say, all the other characters of the piece, make her one of the great figures of all time. She escapes being a monster by her humanity and intense love of life, and by an intelligent doubt of the course which she sees can easily end in her own destruction. But with all her wickedness we can hardly help admiring the old rip, so very alive is she as she trots down the street, swishing her long skirts, her sharp eyes missing nothing, nodding to right and left, always on the lookout for business, and greeted affectionately by one and all as "Mother," "Mistress," or "Old Whore," as the occasion may demand.

Celestina's world is peopled by her own kind, all of them persons in their own right. Sempronio is the perfect foil for his solemn and possessed master, and is, indeed, one of the best of the impudent servants who enliven the pages of Spain's great legacy to the western world, the picaresque. The youth Parmeno is equally well done. He is the wandering student, full of talk, wise saws, and classical tags picked up in the lecture room, vain of his neat syllogisms, torn between loyalty and interest, a foredoomed victim of the vastly superior intelligence of Celestina, who beats him at his own game. Celestina's "daughters" are fitting mates for Sempronio and Parmeno, and provide naughty but hilarious interludes.

Melibea is the conventional, gullible, and innocent girl, haughty and hasty, who catches fire from the maniac frenzy of Calisto. Her inevitable conquest by the old witch and her terrible death are necessary devices for displaying Celestina's gifts to the full. Otherwise, the passion of Calisto and Melibea, or rather the conflict between the two "honors," somehow fails to move us as the author evidently intended. It is a stark and brutal thing, an obsession, powerful enough to give Celestina a reason for being and the reader the illusion of a malignant and inescapable fate. The two lovers are as stiff as the brocaded figures of an ancient tapestry or an old woodcut. They are players in a tragic masque, and their formal attitudes and stilted speech are

appropriate to "love's mournful dance." Indeed, the only truly
pathetic figure among the noble principals is Melibea's father,
Pleberio, whose broken-hearted lament over his daughter's
body, in the last act, suddenly humanizes the masquers. This
may be the place to answer a question that is bound to occur to
the reader: Why doesn't Calisto marry the girl? The answer is
that Don Juan is not the marrying kind. He is a sex-ridden egotist. It is significant that neither Calisto nor Melibea ever enter-
tains the notion of marriage; nor is such a possibility even sug-
gested anywhere. The two lovers are caught in the Dance of
Death and they must tread out its numbers to the end.

The infatuation of Calisto and Melibea has the function of
creating the vortex in which they and all others involved in their
madness are swallowed; but around its edge plays the surpassing
gallery of knaves who, luckily for us, take up a good part of the
story. Celestina is their headmistress. Our interest and sympa-
thies cluster about the game old woman who goes down fighting,
pitting her ingenuity against the senseless brutality of the young
men she has taught too well. This is tragedy in its purest form.
It is also superb art. The death of Celestina is the counterpoint
that gives meaning and poignancy to the others. Celestina has
stature. Her magnificent pride is never broken and she meets her
destiny screaming defiance like a female Lucifer cast into the
abyss.

Why the author chose the dramatic form no one will ever
know. It is quite unlikely that he intended *The Celestina* for the
stage. The long speeches, the philosophizing, the introspection,
would seem to rule out that possibility, although the elements of
a great play are certainly there: a vigorous story, unity of plot,
time, and place, and a manageable number of well-defined characters. The only dramatic narrative the author had to follow was
the classical play, for dialogue, that is. That he was feeling his
way along is, I think, evident enough. The exceedingly long first
act seems to have been written before he had a sharp notion of
what he was about and before he had discovered the potential-
ities in his great central character; but once Celestina begins to

live he wisely lets her go her way with little interference and she writes the book for him.

So I have called *The Celestina* a novel in dialogue. It is the first true novel to appear in the West by a hundred years, as it is assuredly one of the finest. Cervantes, whose debt to it was immense, was a bit shocked by its freedom, but allowed it was "divine" for all that. There is no description, no intervention by the author. The characters reveal themselves and each other, fully and adequately. The reader is plunged into the heart of things at once, sometimes, indeed, with disconcerting abruptness; but the intensity, swiftness of movement, and economy thus achieved more than make up for the absence of confidential chats between author and reader which dilute the novels of later ages.

This is not the place to discuss at length the old question of who or how many wrote *The Celestina*. After several generations of ponderous argument we know as little as we did in the first place, and that little is quickly disposed of. The Burgos edition of 1499 was published anonymously. After 1501 the name of Fernando de Rojas appears in acrostics as the author; but he, or whoever it was, "corrected" the text by interpolating long passages that mercilessly elaborate the obvious, and then, in an apparent attempt to kill the work altogether, he inserted, between the death of Calisto and its discovery by Melibea (who is standing on the other side of the wall from which he falls to his death), five new acts! These additions are not without merit, but I am convinced that the original author could hardly have been a party to the violence thus done to the austere structure of his narrative. In short, all the interpolations and additions are impertinent and obtrusive, and I have omitted them and based my translation on the primitive text.

The author, or, more likely, the early publishers, slavishly imitating Classic models, thought fit to introduce each act with an "argument," which, besides being dull, strikes me as an unnecessary piece of cluttering and I have omitted it. The reason for my choosing the title page of the 1502 edition for an illustration is simple. I should have preferred the title page of the *princeps,* save that the unique copy of it is without one. Anyway, I wanted a beautiful page and found it in the work of the master printer, Jacob Cromberger of Seville.

I have adopted certain conventions to facilitate the reading. Whenever the locale shifts within an act I have broken the act up into scenes. Minor shifts within the same locale I have indicated by spacing, as I have also done to set off dialogues between characters other than the principals in a given scene. The asides or half-heard mumblings which the author makes use of for comic effect and to reveal the thoughts of the secondary characters are set in italics. I have also put in italics the names of eight of the herbs in the inventory of Celestina's witch's shop in the first act which have thus far defied identification. The curious reader will find a learned discussion of the inventory in Julio Cejador y Frauca's edition, vol. 1, pp. 72–86 (*Clásicos Castellanos,* vols. 20, 23. Madrid, 1951).

The sympathetic comments of my friend Warren Ramsey have helped me to clarify many passages. I owe an even greater debt to my wife Marian, whose keen ear and good sense have kept me from wandering too far from my appointed path. To both of them my warm thanks.

LESLEY BYRD SIMPSON

Tragicomedia de
Calisto y melibea.

En la ql se cõtiene de mas de su agra
dable z dulce estilo muchas sentēcias
filosofales:z auisos muy necessarios
pa mãccebos:mostrandoles los enga
ños q estan encerrados en seruientes
z alcahuetas.z nueuamēte añadido
el tractado de Centurio.

Title page of *The Celestina*. Jacob Cromberger. Seville, 1502.
From the copy in the British Museum.

LIST OF CHARACTERS

CALISTO, *a young nobleman*
SEMPRONIO, *his servant*
PARMENO, *his servant*
TRISTRAM, *his servant*
SOSIA, *his servant*

PLEBERIO, *a nobleman*
ALISA, *his wife*
MELIBEA, *his daughter*
LUCRECIA, *her maid*

CELESTINA, *a procuress*
ELICIA, *a prostitute*
AREUSA, *a prostitute*
CRITO, *a pimp*

ACT I

SCENE 1. *Pleberio's garden.*
Calisto, Melibea.

CALISTO. In this, Melibea, I see the goodness of God!

MELIBEA. In what, Calisto?

CALISTO. In His giving nature the power to endow you with such perfect beauty and in granting me, unworthy, the boon of seeing you in this hidden spot where I might declare my secret love. My reward is incomparably greater than I deserve for the services, sacrifices, devotions, and pious works I have offered Him to admit me to this place, for no other power could have done so. What mortal body ever attained such glory! Surely the blessed saints who delight in the Divine Presence know no such happiness! Only, alas!, they and I differ in this: they in their purity enjoy their ecstasy without fear of falling from their lofty eminence, while I in my corruption live in dread of the cruel torment which absence from you will bring.

MELIBEA. Do you consider your reward so great, Calisto?

CALISTO. So great indeed that if God in His heaven were to offer me a seat above His saints I should count it no such felicity!

MELIBEA. Well, if you persist, I'll give you a more fitting reward.

CALISTO. Oh my blessed ears, to hear such words!

MELIBEA. Your unlucky ears, rather, when you hear me out, for your punishment will be as sharp as your mad insolence deserves! Your purpose, Calisto, worthy offspring of such a wit, has come to naught against my virtue! Get out, get out, you obscene scoundrel! It is intolerable that any man should think he might speak to me of the pleasures of unlawful love!

CALISTO. I'll go, but as one whom hateful fortune is determined to destroy!

SCENE 2.   *Calisto's house.*
Calisto, Sempronio.

CALISTO. Sempronio! Sempronio! Sempronio! Where is that accursed rascal?

SEMPRONIO. Here, sir, in the stable.

CALISTO. Why did you leave the room?

SEMPRONIO. The falcon got off his perch and I went to put him back.

CALISTO. The devil take you! May you perish in some sudden calamity or spend eternity in intolerable torment, which I trust will be even more painful than the disastrous death that awaits me! Out, you villain, and make my bed!

SEMPRONIO. Sir, it is done.

CALISTO. Close the shutters and let darkness accompany the wretched and blindness the unlucky! My thoughts are not fit for the light. Oh happy death that comes to the afflicted! If Galen and Hippocrates were living today, could they diagnose my malady? Merciful heaven, fill Pleberio's heart with pity, lest he send this lost and hopeless soul to suffer with the unfortunate Pyramus and the ill-fated Thisbe!

SEMPRONIO. What's the matter?

CALISTO. Get out! Don't speak to me, unless you have a mind to die by these hands before your time!

SEMPRONIO. Very well, I'll go, since you want to weep alone.

CALISTO. The devil go with you!

SEMPRONIO. *How could the devil go with me if he's staying with you? What sudden accident, what evil mischance, has robbed this man of his spirit? And worse yet, of his wits? Shall I leave him or go in to him? If I stay he'll kill me; if I go he'll kill himself. Well, what's it to me? It's better for him to die whose life is a burden than for me who enjoy it. I should stay alive if it's only to see my Elicia again. On the other hand, if he kills himself and I'm the only witness, they'll hold me accountable. I'd better go in. Still, he doesn't want my advice or comfort. It's a sign of death when they don't want to get well. I'll let him fester a while and come to a head. I've heard that it's dangerous to open or press a boil while it's green, for it only gets the more inflamed. I'll leave him alone for a bit. Let him weep who's in pain, for tears and sighs greatly relieve the troubled heart. Besides, if he sees me it will only make him angrier. The sun shines hottest where it's reflected; the eye tires if it hasn't got an object to rest upon, and it gets sharper when it has. I'll wait a bit. If he kills himself meanwhile, well, let him die! Maybe he'll leave me something in his will and change this bad luck of mine. And yet, it's a wicked thing to hope to gain by another's death. Maybe the devil's deceiving me and if he dies I'll be hanged, and that will be the end of Sempronio! On the other hand, wise men say it's a great comfort to the afflicted to have someone to share their troubles, and that a hidden wound is more dangerous. Of these two doubtful extremes it will be better to put up with him and console him. It's possible to get well without method or apparatus, but it's quicker to heal with them.*

CALISTO. Sempronio!

SEMPRONIO. Sir?

CALISTO. Fetch me my lute.

SEMPRONIO. Here it is, sir.

CALISTO (singing). *What pain so great as equals mine!*

SEMPRONIO. Sir, your lute is out of tune.

CALISTO. How can one who is himself out of tune, tune it? How can one who is full of discords have any sense of harmony? Or one whose will is not his own? Or one whose breast is crowded with spur-pricks, peace, war, truce, love, hatred, outrage, worry, suspicion, and all from the same cause? Here, you take the lute and sing me the saddest song you know.

SEMPRONIO (singing).

> *Nero, from the Tarpeian Rock,*
> *Gazed upon burning Rome;*
> *The screams of young and old,*
> *They moved him not!*

CALISTO. The fire that consumes me is greater, and the pity of her of whom I spoke is smaller!

SEMPRONIO. *I was right! This master of mine is crazy!*

CALISTO. What are you muttering there, Sempronio?

SEMPRONIO. Nothing, sir.

CALISTO. Tell me; don't be afraid.

SEMPRONIO. I was saying, sir, how can a fire be greater that torments only one living being than one that burns a whole city and such multitudes of people?

CALISTO. How? I'll tell you. Greater is the fire that lasts for eighty years than one that passes in a day, and greater is the fire that kills a soul than one that burns a hundred thousand bodies. There's as great a difference between appearance and reality, between a living thing and its painted counterfeit, as there is between the fire you speak of and the one that's consuming me! If Purgatory is as bad as this, I'd rather my soul went to oblivion with the dumb brutes than to heaven by such a means!

SEMPRONIO. *I said it! This business isn't going to stop here! He's not only mad, but a heretic!*

CALISTO. Haven't I told you to speak up? What are you saying?

SEMPRONIO. I was saying, God forbid!, for what you've just said is a kind of heresy.

CALISTO. What's that got to do with me?

SEMPRONIO. Aren't you a Christian?

CALISTO. Me? I'm a Melibean! I worship Melibea! I believe in Melibea! I love Melibea!

SEMPRONIO. *It's your funeral. Melibea's too big for my master to hold down and she comes spewing up out of his mouth. But enough of this.* I know what's ailing you. I'll cure you.

CALISTO. Impossible!

SEMPRONIO. On the contrary, it's easy. The beginning of a cure is to recognize the disease.

CALISTO. How can you put order into something that has no order?

SEMPRONIO. *Ho, ho, ho! So this is the fire that consumes Calisto? These are his troubles? Does he think that love shoots his arrows at him alone? Almighty God, how deep are Thy mysteries! What force didst Thou give to love that it should create such disturbance in a lover? How rarely didst Thou set a limit to it! The lover thinks he's left behind in the race. All others pass him; all break away like swift bulls which, pricked and stung with darts, leap over the barriers. Thou didst command man to leave father and mother for his wife; but now they do not only that, but abandon Thy law, as Calisto does. But I'm not astonished, for wise men, saints, and prophets have forgotten Thee for love.*

CALISTO. Sempronio?

SEMPRONIO. Sir?

CALISTO. Don't leave me.

SEMPRONIO. *This bagpipe's playing another tune!*

CALISTO. What do you think of this sickness of mine?

SEMPRONIO. You're in love with Melibea. But it's a sad thing to see you held captive by one lone woman.

CALISTO. You know little of constancy.

SEMPRONIO. Perseverance in evil is not constancy; rather, in my country they call it stubbornness or pig-headedness. You philosophers of Cupid may call it what you will.

CALISTO. It's à wicked thing to lie when you pretend to be teaching another. Don't you praise your mistress Elicia?

SEMPRONIO. Follow my good advice and not my bad example.

CALISTO. What fault in me are you reproving?

SEMPRONIO. That you're submitting your man's dignity to the frailty of a woman.

CALISTO. A woman, you clod? A goddess!

SEMPRONIO. Do you really believe that, or are you making game of me?

CALISTO. Making game of you? I believe in her as I believe in God, and I say there's no higher sovereign in heaven!

SEMPRONIO. Ha, ha, ha! Did you ever hear such blasphemy? Or see such blindness?

CALISTO. What are you laughing about?

SEMPRONIO. I'm laughing because I don't think worse sins were invented even in Sodom!

CALISTO. How's that?

SEMPRONIO. The Sodomites tried to commit abominations with unknown angels, but you with one you hold to be a goddess!

CALISTO. Damn you! You've made me laugh, a thing I hadn't expected to do this year.

SEMPRONIO. Oh come! Were you going to weep the rest of your life?

CALISTO. Yes.

SEMPRONIO. Why?

CALISTO. Because I love one I'm unworthy of, one I cannot hope to possess.

SEMPRONIO. *Oh the cowardly son of a whore! What a Nimrod, what an Alexander the Great, who thought themselves worthy, not only to rule the world, but heaven as well!*

CALISTO. I didn't hear you. Say that again.

SEMPRONIO. I was saying that you, who are braver than Nimrod or Alexander, despair of possessing a mere woman. Why, many women of great estate have submitted themselves to the embraces and stinking breaths of vile muleteers, and others to brute beasts! Haven't you read of Pasiphae and the bull? Or of Minerva and the dog?

CALISTO. Those are old wives' tales. I don't believe them.

SEMPRONIO. Was that affair of your grandmother and the ape an old wives' tale? Your grandfather's knife is my witness!

CALISTO. Curse this fool! How he babbles!

SEMPRONIO. Did I pink you? Read your histories; study your philosophers; read your poets. Their books are full of stories of wicked women who destroyed men, men who like yourself held them in high esteem. Listen to Solomon where he says that women and wine make men deny God. Take counsel with Seneca and you'll see what *he* thinks of them. Consult Aristotle or St. Bernard. Gentiles, Jews, Christians, and Moors are all of one mind in this. Not that what they say is true of all women, for there are, and have been, many saintly, virtuous, and noble women whose shining crowns belie the general opinion. But the others! Who could tell you their lies, their tricks, their changes, their fickleness, their sniveling, their bad temper, their impu-

dence? Their deceits, their gossiping, their ingratitude, their
inconstancy, their presumption, their boastfulness, their false
humility, their folly, their scorn, their servility, their gluttony,
their lust, their filth, their cowardice, their insolence, their
sorcery, their gibes, their scolding, their want of shame, their
whoring? Consider the giddy little brains concealed behind
those long and delicate veils! Or within those fine and sumptu-
ous gowns! What corruption, what cesspools, beneath those
gaudy temples! They are called limbs of Satan, the fountainhead
of sin, and the destroyers of Paradise. Haven't you read in St.
John, where he says: "This is woman, the ancient curse that
drove Adam out of the delights of Eden; she it was who sent the
human race to hell; she it was whom the prophet Elijah re-
buked?" And so on.

CALISTO. Tell me then; this Adam, this Solomon, this David, this
Aristotle, this Virgil, all those you name, how is it they succumbed to women? Am I stronger than they?

SEMPRONIO. I would have you imitate those who conquered
women, not those who were conquered by them. Fly their tricks!
Why, don't you know what they do? Things you'd hardly believe! They have no method, no reason, no purpose. They offer
themselves to men because they can't help themselves. They let
you in through a hole in the wall and then insult you in the
street. They invite, they dismiss, they beckon, they ignore. They
make you think they love you, and it turns out they hate you.
They're quick to anger and quick to make peace. They expect
you to guess what's in their mind. What a plague, what an an-
noyance, what a bore it is to be with them longer than that brief
moment when they're disposed to love!

CALISTO. Go away! The more you say against her and the more
obstacles you put in my way, the more I love her. I don't understand it.

SEMPRONIO. My advice, I'm beginning to see, is wasted on children who won't listen to reason and who can't govern themselves.

CALISTO. What do you know about it? Who taught you all this?

SEMPRONIO. Who? Why, they themselves! Once they've revealed themselves to men they lose all sense of shame and teach you this and a great deal more besides. Weigh yourself on the scales of honor and strive to be more worthy than you're reputed to be. It's a worse folly for a man to fall from his proper station of his own doing than to raise himself to a higher place than he deserves.

CALISTO. What's all that got to do with me? Who am I?

SEMPRONIO. Who? First of all you're a man! Moreover, a man of wit endowed with nature's best gifts, namely, beauty, grace, a fine body, strength, and agility. Besides, she shared her wealth with you so liberally that your inward gifts shine no less brightly than those without. Lacking these outward gifts, of which fortune is mistress, no one in this life can be fortunate. Finally, you were born under such a lucky star that everyone loves you.

CALISTO. But not Melibea! In everything you've said of me, Sempronio, Melibea is beyond compare my better. Consider the nobility and antiquity of her family, her great patrimony, her excellent wit, her shining virtue, her high and ineffable grace, her sovereign beauty; and of this I beg you to let me speak a little for my comfort; but I'll speak only of those parts that are visible to the eye, for if I could speak of what is hidden, it would be useless for us to exchange these miserable words!

SEMPRONIO. *What lies and idiocies will this benighted master of mine utter now?*

CALISTO. What are you saying?

SEMPRONIO. I said, say on, for I'll greatly enjoy hearing you. *And may God reward you as I'll enjoy your sermon!*

CALISTO. What?

SEMPRONIO. I said, may God bless me as I'll be pleased to hear it!

CALISTO. Well then, just to please you, I'll describe her to you in detail.

SEMPRONIO. *God help us! I'm in for it! But his fit won't last forever!*

CALISTO. I'll begin with the hairs of her head. Have you ever by chance seen the skeins of golden threads they spin in Araby? Hers are more beautiful and shine no less. They reach to the very soles of her feet. And then, when they're curled and tied with a fine ribbon, as she wears them, they turn men into stones!

SEMPRONIO. *Into asses, rather!*

CALISTO. What's that?

SEMPRONIO. I said her hairs could hardly resemble asses' bristles.

CALISTO. What a vile figure! What an idiot!

SEMPRONIO. *If I'm an idiot, what is he?*

CALISTO. Her eyes, green and wide; her lashes, long; her brows, dainty and high; her nose, neither too large nor too small; her mouth, little; her teeth, small and white; her lips, red and plump; her face, somewhat longer than it is round; her bosom, high; her breasts, so full and firm, who can describe them? How a man will stretch himself when he sees them! Her skin, smooth and lustrous, and so white it darkens the snow; her color, varied, as she would have chosen it for herself. . . .

SEMPRONIO. *This fool has got the bit in his teeth!*

CALISTO. Her hands, small, but not too small, and sweetly fleshed; her fingers, long; her nails likewise, and so pink they seem like rubies among pearls. And from what I could see of her hidden parts, she's incomparably fairer than the most beautiful of the goddesses whom Paris judged!

SEMPRONIO. Have you done?

CALISTO. As briefly as I could.

SEMPRONIO. Well, even if everything you say of her is true, you, being a man, are still more worthy.

CALISTO. How's that?

SEMPRONIO. Because she is imperfect and in her imperfection she desires and lusts after you. Haven't you read what the philosophers say, that as matter desires form, so woman desires man?

CALISTO. Wretch that I am! When will Melibea desire me?

SEMPRONIO. It could happen, even though you hated her as much as you love her now, and when you possessed her you'd see her with eyes cured of their present squint.

CALISTO. With what kind of eyes?

SEMPRONIO. With clear eyes.

CALISTO. And how do I see her now?

SEMPRONIO. Through a magnifying glass, which makes everything seem bigger than it is. . . . However, to keep you from despair I'll undertake to get her for you.

CALISTO. May God reward you! Even though I don't believe you, it's wonderful to hear!

SEMPRONIO. On the contrary, I'll certainly do it.

CALISTO. God bless you! That brocaded doublet I wore yesterday, take it, Sempronio, it's yours!

SEMPRONIO. *And God bless you for it and for the many more you're going to give me! I've got the best of this joke! A few prods like that and I'll bring her to his very bed! I'm on the right track! My master's gift did it! If you want to get something done you've got to pay for it!*

CALISTO. Don't be lazy now!

SEMPRONIO. Don't *you* be! A lazy master can't have a diligent servant.

CALISTO. How do you plan to go about this pious work?

SEMPRONIO. I'll tell you. A good many days ago I met, out toward the edge of this quarter, a bewhiskered old beldame who calls herself Celestina, a witch, astute and wise in all evil things. They say the number of maidenheads broken and repaired under her authority in this city passes five thousand. She can move the very stones to lechery if she sets her mind to it!

CALISTO. Could I see her?

SEMPRONIO. I'll bring her to you. Be cordial and liberal with her, and while I'm gone cook up a good story, so she'll prescribe the proper medicine for you.

CALISTO. Well, what are you waiting for?

SEMPRONIO. I'm off, and God be with you!

CALISTO. And may He guide your steps! . . . Almighty and everlasting God, Thou who guidest the lost and led'st the Orient Kings to Bethlehem by the star, and by it led'st them back again, humbly I beseech Thee to guide my Sempronio in such wise that he may change my sorrow into gladness and bring me my heart's desire!

SCENE 3. *Celestina's house. Celestina, Sempronio, Elicia, Crito.*

CELESTINA. Good news, Elicia! It's Sempronio! Sempronio!

ELICIA. Hush!

CELESTINA. Why?

ELICIA. Crito's with me.

CELESTINA. Hide him in the broom closet! Quickly now! Tell him your cousin's coming!

ELICIA. Crito, hide in here! My cousin's coming! I'm ruined!

CRITO. It's all right. Don't worry about me.

SEMPRONIO. My blessed mother! How I've missed you!

CELESTINA. My son! My king! You've upset me quite! I can't speak! Kiss me again! Three whole days away? How could you? Elicia, Elicia, look who's here!

ELICIA. Who, mother?

CELESTINA. Sempronio!

ELICIA. Oh dear! How my heart is thumping! How is he?

CELESTINA. Come and see for yourself. He's here. But I'll kiss him, not you!

ELICIA. Oh you accursed traitor! I hope you die of ulcers and tumors, or that your enémies kill you, or you get hanged for your wicked crimes! Oh, oh!

SEMPRONIO. Ho, ho, ho! What's the matter with my Elicia? What's eating you?

ELICIA. Three days without coming round? Be damned to you! What a poor fool I was for trusting you!

SEMPRONIO. Hush, my dear. Do you think that distance can quench the fire, the deep love in my heart? You're always with me, wherever I go. Don't torture yourself as I've been tortured. . . . But tell me, whose footsteps do I hear upstairs?

ELICIA. It's one of my lovers!

SEMPRONIO. I believe you!

ELICIA. By my faith, it's true! Go up and see for yourself!

SEMPRONIO. I will.

CELESTINA. Come, come! Pay no attention to the silly thing. She's all upset by your neglect. She'll say anything. Come here and talk to me. Let's not waste time.

SEMPRONIO. But who is upstairs?

CELESTINA. Do you really want to know?

SEMPRONIO. Yes.

CELESTINA. It's a girl that a friar left with me.

SEMPRONIO. What friar?

CELESTINA. Don't ask.

SEMPRONIO. On my life, mother, what friar?

CELESTINA. Do you insist? The fat one.

SEMPRONIO. Oh the poor girl, and what a load she's going to carry!

CELESTINA. We all have to carry one, but you haven't seen many saddle galls on a horse's belly, have you?

SEMPRONIO. Maybe not saddle galls, but heel prints a-plenty!

CELESTINA. You wag!

SEMPRONIO. Never mind my being a wag and show me the girl.

ELICIA. You lout! So you want to see her, do you? I hope your eyes pop out when you do! You're not satisfied with one, but you want us both? Go up and see her and never let me see your face again!

SEMPRONIO. Hush! My goodness, and did she get angry with me? I don't want to see that girl or any woman alive. Leave us now, for I've got business with our mother.

ELICIA. Get out, you stranger! Go away and stay three more years, and don't come back!

SEMPRONIO. Mother, you must trust me and believe I'm serious. Get your shawl and come with me. I've got some good news for you that I'll explain on the way. It would cost us money if I took the time to explain things here.

CELESTINA. Good-bye, Elicia! Lock the door. Good-bye, my house!

SCENE 4. *A street.   Celestina, Sempronio.*

SEMPRONIO. Now, dear mother, put everything else out of your mind and listen to me. Don't let your attention wander off in all directions, for he who puts his mind on many things keeps it on nothing. You'll gather my meaning from my words. But first I want you to know something about me, and that is, that ever since I put my trust in you I've never desired any good thing for myself without wishing to share it with you.

CELESTINA. May God be good to you, my son, if only for your charity toward this sinful old woman! But speak plainly; don't hold back. We know each other too well to have need of preambles and corollaries and beating about the bush. Come to the point, for it's foolish to say in many words what can be understood in few.

SEMPRONIO. You're right. Well, it's this. Calisto is burning up with love of Melibea and he needs our help. And, since he needs us both, let's both make something out of it. What makes men prosperous is to recognize the proper moment and take advantage of it.

CELESTINA. I see what you mean. All you need to do with me is tip me a wink. I mean I'm as pleased over your good news as a surgeon is over a broken head, and just as a surgeon will inflame a wound in order to prolong the treatment, so shall I do with Calisto and keep him uncertain of his cure. As the saying goes, hope deferred maketh the heart sick, so the more hopeless he gets, the more we'll promise him. Do you follow me?

SEMPRONIO. Quiet now! We're at his door and, as they say, the walls have ears.

CELESTINA. Knock.

SEMPRONIO. (Knocks.)

SCENE 5. *Calisto's house. Calisto, Parmeno, Sempronio, Celestina.*

CALISTO. Parmeno!

PARMENO. Sir?

CALISTO. Are you deaf, you accursed dummy?

PARMENO. What is it, sir?

CALISTO. Someone's knocking at the door! Run!

PARMENO. Who's there?

SEMPRONIO. Open the door for me and this good old lady.

PARMENO. Sir, Sempronio and an old painted whore were making all that racket.

CALISTO. Silence, you villain! She's my aunt! Run and open! I've always noticed that when a man flies from one danger he runs into a worse one. To cover up this mistake of Parmeno, who spoke out of love or fidelity or fear, I've fallen into the bad graces of her who has no less power over my life than God himself!

PARMENO. What's the hurry, sir? Why are you worried? Do you think she was insulted by the name I called her? Don't believe it! Why, she puffs up as much when she hears it as you do when someone says: "What a fine horseman is Calisto!" Besides, that's her proper title and the one she goes by. If she's among a hundred women and someone says "Old Whore!," with no embarrassment whatever she turns her head and answers with smiling face. At parties, festivals, weddings, guild meetings, funerals, at every kind of gathering, she's the center of merriment. If she walks among dogs, that's the name they bark. If it's birds, they sing nothing else. If it's a flock of sheep, they bleat her name. If it's asses, they bray "Old Whore!" The very frogs in their puddles croak it. If she passes a smithy, the smiths' hammers pound it out. Carpenters and armorers, farriers, tinkers, and fullers— every kind of instrument fills the air with her name. Farmers in their fields, at their plowing, in the vineyards, or at harvest, lighten their labors with her. When gamblers lose at the gaming table, then you should hear her praises ring forth! All things that make a noise, wherever she is, proclaim her. Oh what a consumer of roasted eggs her husband was! What else would you know, save that when one stone strikes against another, together they cry "Old Whore!"

CALISTO. How do you know all this?

PARMENO. I'll tell you. Many years ago my mother, who was a poor woman, dwelt in her neighborhood, and this Celestina begged me of her for a servant, although she doesn't know me now, for I worked for her only a short time and I've changed a good deal.

CALISTO. What did you do?

PARMENO. Sir, I went to market with her and carried her provisions and did such other chores as my tender strength would allow. But in the short month I was with her I learned things I've never forgotten! This good woman used to have, on the outskirts of town near the tanneries, a house somewhat removed from the street, half tumbled-down, badly repaired and worse furnished. She had six trades, to wit: laundress, perfumer, a master hand at making cosmetics and replacing damaged maidenheads, procuress, and something of a witch. Her first trade was a cover for the rest, and with this excuse many servant girls went to her house to do their washing. None of them came without a sausage, or some wheat or flour, or a jug of wine, or provisions stolen from their mistresses. And many other little thefts were there concealed. She was a great friend of students, purveyors, and priests' servants, and sold them the innocent blood of those poor girls which they had foolishly risked for the repair she had promised them. She flew even higher and through her girls reached the most sheltered females, this on honest occasions, such as the Stations of the Cross, nocturnal processions, early Mass, and other secret devotions. I've seen many such enter her house, their faces covered, with men behind them, barefoot, penitent, muffled, their shoes unlatched, who were going there to do penance for their sins! You can't imagine the traffic she carried on. She was a baby doctor; she picked up flax in one house and brought it to be spun in another—all this as an excuse to get in everywhere. One would say, "Mother, come here!" Another, "Mother, go there!" Or, "There goes the old woman!" Or, "Here comes the mistress!" Everyone knew her. And yet, in spite of her many duties, she always found time to go to Mass or vespers; nor did she neglect the monasteries and nunneries, where she peddled her sweetcakes and her services.

In her house she manufactured perfumes and counterfeited storax, benjamin, anime, amber, civet, powders, and musk. She had a room full of retorts and flasks, with vessels of earthenware, glass, tin, and brass, of a thousand different shapes. There she made mercury sublimate, skin lotions, jars of ointment, and eyebrow pencils; skin-fillers, salves, cleansers, fresheners, clarifiers, bleaches, and other waters for the face; grated asphodel, senna pods, tarragon, gall, new wine, and must, all distilled and sweetened with sugar. For softening the skin she used lemon juice, turpeth, deer and heron marrow, and other confections. She made perfume from roses, orange flowers, jasmine, clover, honeysuckle, and carnations, all powdered and mixed with musk and wine. For bleaching the hair she made rinses of vine shoots, holm oak, rye, and horehound, with saltpetre, alum, yarrow, and sundry other ingredients. It would be tiresome to recite all the oils and fats she extracted: from cows, bears, camels, snakes, rabbits, whales, herons, bitterns, chamois, wild cats, badgers, squirrels, porcupines, and otters. It would astonish you to learn of all the things she used for her medicinal baths, with herbs and roots which she had hanging from her roof, to wit: camomile, rosemary, marshmallow, maiden's hair, melilot, alder, mustard, lavender, white laurel, *tortarosa, gramonilla, flor salvaje,* psoralea, *pico de oro,* and *hoja tinta.* The oils she used for the face you would hardly believe: storax, jasmine, lemon, melon seed, benjamin, pistachio, pine nut, grape seed, jubejube nut, fennel, lupine, vetch, *carilla,* and chickweed. She also kept a bit of balsam in a flask with which she used to treat that scar she has across her face. For the repair of maidenheads she used bladders, or she stitched them up. In a small painted box on a platform she kept a supply of furrier's needles and waxed silk, and hanging under it she had roots of *hojaplasma* and *fuste sanguino,* squill, and horsetail. She did wonders with all this apparatus. When the French ambassador was here, why, she sold him one of her girls for a virgin three times running!

CALISTO. Too bad it wasn't a hundred!

PARMENO. Holy God, yes! Besides, out of charity she took care of many orphans and shut-ins who gave themselves into her hands. In another room she kept her love philtres made of the bones from stags' hearts, serpents' tongues, partridge heads, asses' brains, cauls of new-born foals, babies' fat, French beans, lodestones, the rope of a hanged man, ivy flowers, hedgehog bristles, badgers' feet, fern seeds, the stone from an eagle's nest, and a thousand other things.

Numbers of men and women came to see her. From some she demanded a bit of the bread they had nibbled; from others, a garment; from others, a strand of hair. On the hands of some she wrote letters in saffron, on others, in vermillion. To some she gave hearts of wax stuck full of broken needles, or images made of clay or lead, very horrible to see. She would paint figures on the ground and speak words over them. In short, who could tell you all the things this old woman did? And it was nothing but lies and mockery.

CALISTO. Very well, Parmeno. Leave the rest for some other time. You've told me enough for the present and I'm obliged to you. But let's not keep her waiting any longer. After all, I invited her to come and we've kept her too long already. And I beg you, Parmeno, not to let your envy of Sempronio interfere with what he's doing for me. He's serving me well. I gave him a doublet, but I'll give you a coat. And don't think I despise your counsel. Things spiritual take precedence over things temporal; the beast of burden works harder than a man and is fed and cared for, but not as a friend. That's how you stand with me as against Sempronio. Keep this to yourself, but I think of you as my equal and my friend.

PARMENO. It grieves me, sir, after your offer and advice, to see you doubting my service and my loyalty. When did you ever see me envious, sir, or put my own interest or resentments above your welfare?

CALISTO. Don't feel badly, Parmeno. Your good manners and courtesy raise you in my esteem above all my servants; but in this difficult case, in which my health and life are at stake, I must provide for all contingencies. Your gentleness is the fruit of a good nature, just as a good nature is the foundation of excellence. But enough of this. Let's go down and see our physician.

CELESTINA. I hear footsteps. Someone's coming down. Let on you don't hear it, Sempronio. Just keep still and let me say what needs to be said.

SEMPRONIO. Very well, talk.

CELESTINA. Don't plague me! Don't insist! It's like spurring a tired horse to put so much on me. You take your master's troubles so hard that one would think you were he, and he, you, and that you have but one body between you. You may be sure that I didn't come here to fail him in his suit. I'll succeed or die in the attempt!

CALISTO. Be quiet now, Parmeno, and listen to what they're saying. Let's see what they're up to. . . . Oh wonderful woman! Oh worldly goods, unworthy of being possessed by such a high heart! Oh my true and faithful Sempronio! Did you hear, my

Parmeno? Was I right? What do you say now, you keeper of my secrets, my dear counsellor?

PARMENO. I protest my innocence of your first suspicion and I'll speak to you loyally as a friend, since you granted me that honor. Listen to me, sir, and don't let your mind be dulled by love or blinded by the thought of pleasure to come. Be patient, not hasty. Don't be so anxious to hit the bull's eye that you miss the target altogether. I may be young, but I've seen a good deal, and good sense and the sight of many things have ripened my experience. These two have either seen you or heard you coming down the stairs, and they've trumped up this little comedy for your benefit.

SEMPRONIO. I don't like what Parmeno's saying, not a bit!

CELESTINA. Hush, for by my sainted mother wherever the ass goes he'll wear his pack-saddle! You leave Parmeno to me and I'll make him one of us. We'll give him a share of whatever we earn. We'll all make money; we'll all share it; we'll all be happy together. I'll bring him to you tamed and gentle and eating out of my hand, and we'll all three ride that donkey!

CALISTO. Sempronio!

SEMPRONIO. Sir?

CALISTO. Why are you waiting out there, you who hold the key to my life? Open the door! . . . Oh Parmeno, I see her! I am well! I live again! Mark what a reverend person she is! What modesty! Inward goodness usually shows in one's face. Oh virtuous old age! Oh aged virtue! Oh glorious hope of my desired purpose! Oh purpose of my happy hope! Oh relief of my suffering, end of my torment, my regeneration, my new life, my resurrection! Let me approach and kiss those healing hands! But I'm unworthy! Let me kneel, rather, and worship the ground you walk upon and kiss it out of reverence for you!

CELESTINA. Sempronio, I live on words! The old bones I've gnawed, this silly master of yours thinks he can give me to eat!

Well, I've got something else in store for him which he'll discover when he begins to fry! Tell him to shut his mouth and open his purse, for I don't even trust his deeds, much less his words. Ho, I'll curry you, you lame ass! You should have got up earlier in the morning!

PARMENO. *Woe to the ears that hear such words! Oh unlucky Calisto, beaten and blind! Kneeling down and worshipping the most ancient and whorish piece of earth that ever rubbed her shoulders in the stews! He's undone, conquered, fallen! Beyond redemption, counsel, or effort!*

CALISTO. What was our mother saying, Sempronio. Does she think I'm offering her words instead of money?

SEMPRONIO. That's what I gathered.

CALISTO. Come with me, then. Bring the keys and I'll end her doubt.

SEMPRONIO. You'll do well. Let's go at once. Weeds shouldn't be allowed to grow in the wheat or suspicions in the hearts of friends, but should be instantly cleared out with the hoe of good works.

CALISTO. Wisely said. Come at once.

CELESTINA. Parmeno, I'm glad of this chance to show you how much I love you and what you mean to me, although you're not worthy of it. And I say not worthy because of what I heard you say just now; but I'll not hold it against you, for virtue advises us to suffer temptations and not to repay evil with evil, especially when we are tempted by youths not well taught in the things of this world and who with foolish loyalty ruin themselves and their masters, as you are doing with Calisto. I heard you well enough! Don't think I've lost my hearing in my old age along with my other external senses! I understand not only what I see and hear, but I read your most intimate thoughts with the eyes of the mind. . . . You must know, Parmeno, that your master is sick with love; but don't judge him to be a weakling on that account, for love conquers all things. And know, if you don't know it already, that these two propositions are true: first, that of necessity man must love woman, and woman, man; second, that he who truly loves is necessarily troubled by the sweetness of that sovereign delight which was ordained by the Maker of all things in order to perpetuate mankind, and without which mankind would perish from the earth. Not only the human race, but the fishes, the beasts, the birds, and the reptiles have this attribute, and even in the vegetable kingdom some plants have it if they are placed near together, and they are male and female, as we know by the authority of herbalists and husbandmen. What do you say to that, my Parmeno, my little fool, my silly one, my angel, my pearl, my little simpleton? Making faces at me? Come here, little bugger! You know nothing of the world and its pleasures. Damn me if I'd let you come near me, old as I am, for your voice is getting deep and your beard is sprouting! I'll bet the point of your belly is anything but quiet!

PARMENO. It's like the tail of a scorpion!

CELESTINA. Worse! A scorpion's sting causes no swelling, but yours leaves your victims swollen for nine months!

PARMENO. He, he, he!

CELESTINA. Do you laugh, my little carbuncle?

PARMENO. Hush, mother. Don't blame me or take me for a fool, even though I'm young. I love Calisto because I owe him my loyalty and because he has taken care of me and given me gifts, and honored and treated me well, which is a strong link, for the love of the servant for the service of his master binds him, just as the contrary releases him. I see him lost, for there's nothing worse than to desire without hope, especially since he thinks to conclude his difficult affair with the vain advice and foolish arguments of that jackass Sempronio, which is like trying to dig out mites with a spade and pickaxe! I can't stand it; it makes me weep.

CELESTINA. Parmeno, don't you see it's folly or simplicity to weep over what can't be helped by weeping?

PARMENO. But that's why I'm weeping! If it were possible to help my master by weeping, my pleasure would be so great that I couldn't weep! As it is, I have no hope or joy, and I weep.

CELESTINA. You're wasting your tears over what you can't prevent. And don't think you can cure him. Hasn't this ever happened to anyone else, Parmeno?

PARMENO. Yes, but I don't like to see my master suffer.

CELESTINA. He isn't suffering and, even if he is, he can be cured.

PARMENO. I'm not convinced. In the doing of good the act is better than the potentiality; in evil the potentiality is better than the act. Thus it's better to be well than to be able to be well, and to be potentially ill is better than to be ill in fact.

CELESTINA. You rascal! As if I didn't see through you! Don't you know what's the matter with him? What are you complaining of? Very well, then, have your little joke, turn things upside down and believe what you will, but he's sick and his cure is in the hands of this weak old woman.

PARMENO. You mean in the hands of this weak old whore!

CELESTINA. The devil take you, you little villain! How dare you talk to me like that?

PARMENO. Why, I know you!

CELESTINA. Who are you?

PARMENO. Who? I'm Parmeno, the son of Albert your gossip, and I spent a month at your house when my mother left me with you, while you were living on the bank of the river near the tanneries.

CELESTINA. Jesus, Mary, and Joseph! You are Parmeno, the son of Claudina?

PARMENO. The same!

CELESTINA. Well, may you burn in hell, for your mother was as much of an old whore as myself! What have you got against me, Parmeno? It's he, it's he, by all the saints! Come to me! Why, many's the spanking I've given you in this world, and as many kisses! Don't you remember when you slept at my feet, little rogue?

PARMENO. I do indeed! And sometimes, even though I was only a baby, you'd pull me up to the head of the bed and squeeze me, and I'd run away because you stank so of old age!

CELESTINA. Damn the impudent rascal! But that's enough joking. Hear me now, my son, and listen. I was called here for one purpose, but I came for another, and, even though I pretended not to know you, you were the real cause of it. My son, you well know that your mother (may she rest in peace!) left you with me while your father was still living. Well, after you went away he died for no other reason than the anxiety he felt about your future, and because of your absence his last years were full of care and anguish. At the time he passed from this life he sent for me and gave you secretly into my charge, and, with no other witness but Him who knows all our deeds and thoughts and who scrutinizes our hearts and bowels, he made me swear I'd search you out and shelter you, and then, when you should be older and wiser, he bade me show you where he had buried a great store of gold and silver, a larger fortune than that of your master Calisto. I gave him my word and he died consoled. And since a promise given to the dead, who cannot act for themselves, is more sacred than that given to the living, I spent a great deal of time and money looking for you, until it pleased Him who bears all our burdens and answers all our just demands and directs our pious works, to let me find you here where only three days ago I learned you were living. You've caused me plenty of grief wandering friendless through so many lands. As Seneca says, wanderers have many dwelling places but few friends, for they have no time to make them. He who lives in many places rests in none; nor can food which is thrown up as soon as eaten do one any good; nor is there anything more damaging to the health than diversity, change, and variety of diet. That wound is never closed which is treated with many medicines; nor does that plant ever flourish which is often removed; nor is there anything so profitable that it yields a profit as soon as it arrives.

Therefore, my son, leave off these youthful follies and listen to reason and the voice of your elders. Settle down, and where better than in my good will and in my heart and care, where your parents left you? And, speaking as your true mother, on pain of the curse that your parents put on you if you should disobey me, I charge you to put up with this master of yours for the present and serve him until I advise you differently, but not with foolish loyalty, thinking you can build firmly upon such a shaky foundation—for that's what these fine gentlemen are nowadays. Win friends, for friends are durable, and be loyal to them. Don't live on air. Forget the empty words of masters who destroy the substance of their servants with vain and hollow promises. Like leeches they suck your blood. They don't thank you; they insult you. They forget your services and neglect to pay you. Woe to him who grows old in a palace! As is written of the Pool of Bethesda, of every hundred who entered it, only one was cured. Masters these days love themselves more than the servants in their house. And they're right! Their servants should do the same. Gifts, generosity, and noble deeds are things of the past. All these masters use their servants basely and meanly for their own ends; and their servants, even those in the lower ranks, should do no less and live by their own law.

I say all this, Parmeno my son, because this master of yours strikes me as a fool-killer. He wants to be served, but he doesn't want to pay for it. Keep your eyes open and you'll see I'm right. Make friends for yourself in his house, for friends are the best treasure in the world; but don't try to be your master's friend, for friendship is rarely possible between different ranks and fortunes. We've got a case in hand, as you know, in which we all stand to make something and you to better yourself. So much for the present. Everything else I told you can wait for the proper occasion. Meanwhile, do you make friends with Sempronio for your own good.

PARMENO. Celestina, your words make me tremble. I don't know what to do. I'm puzzled. I owe you my love as a mother, but I owe Calisto my love as a master. I'd like to be rich, but he who climbs by foul means falls more quickly than he climbed. I don't want any ill-won wealth.

CELESTINA. Well, I do! I'm for my own people, right or wrong!

PARMENO. I'd not be happy with it. Contented poverty, to my mind, is an honest thing. I say more, that they are not poor who have little, but they who desire much. No matter what you say, therefore, I can't believe you in this. I want to be able to live my life without envy, cross deserts and the wilderness without fear, sleep without startings, answer my detractors, suffer violence without dishonor, and meet oppression with resistance.

CELESTINA. Oh my son, it is well said that prudence comes only with old age, and you are very young.

PARMENO. It's better to live in carefree poverty, I say.

CELESTINA. Say, rather, like a grown man, that fortune favors the bold. Besides, what person of wealth in the republic would choose to live without friends? You, praise God!, have wealth. Don't you know that you need friends to preserve it? And don't think that the protection of your master makes you secure, for the greater your fortune, the less secure it is. So when trouble comes your only recourse is your friends. And where can you find this security except in the three pursuits in which friendships are sealed, namely, in virtue, profit, and pleasure? In virtue, see how much you and Sempronio are alike in it. As for profit, it's in your own hands if you will work with him. And pleasure? The same, for you're both at that time of life when you're ready for every kind. Young men join in it more than the old, that is, in gaming, dressing, jesting, eating and drinking, love-making, and good company. . . . Ah Parmeno, if you only would, what a life we could have! . . . . Sempronio loves Elicia, Areusa's cousin.

PARMENO. Areusa's cousin?

women = motivating factor, move all action along

CELESTINA. No other.

PARMENO. Do you mean Areusa, Eliso's daughter?

CELESTINA. The very same.

PARMENO. Sure?

CELESTINA. Sure.

PARMENO. By all that's wonderful!

CELESTINA. Well, do you like the idea?

PARMENO. It's marvelous!

CELESTINA. You're in luck, then, for here's the hand that can get her for you.

PARMENO. Upon my word, mother, I can't believe anyone any more!

CELESTINA. It's folly to believe everyone and an error to believe no one.

PARMENO. I mean, I believe you, but I don't dare. Please leave me!

CELESTINA. Oh you poor creature! It's a faint heart that doesn't open the door to fortune when she knocks. God gives sweetmeats to those who've got no teeth to chew them! Oh you simpleton! You must think that the greater your understanding and discretion are, the less luck you'll have. It's an idle saying.

PARMENO. Oh Celestina, I've heard my elders say that one example of lechery or avarice does a great deal of harm, and that a man should associate only with those who will make him better and avoid those he'll have to improve. Sempronio will not make me better by his example, nor will I be able to cure his vices. . . .

CELESTINA. You talk like a fool! No good thing can be enjoyed without company. Don't shrink back and pull a long face. Nature dislikes gloom and rejoices in cheerfulness. Pleasure can be had only with friends in things of the senses, and especially in telling one another your adventures in love. I did this! He told me that! We played such and such a trick! I seized her thus! I kissed her thus! She bit me thus! I embraced her thus! She yielded thus! What talk! What fun! What games! What kisses! Let's go yonder! Let's go back! Let the music play! Let's cap verses! Let's sing songs! Let's make up stories! There she goes to Mass! She'll be out again tomorrow! Let's stroll past her house! Look, here's a note from her! Hold the ladder for me! Watch the door! Oh the poor cuckold, he's left her alone! Let's have another try at her! . . . . Ah Parmeno, is there any pleasure without company? By my faith, I know what I'm talking about! This only is pleasure, for that other business is better done by the asses in the field!

PARMENO. I shouldn't let myself be persuaded by promises of pleasure, like those who have succumbed to heretical teachings wrapped up in sweet poison for trapping the wills of the weak, or like those others who have blinded the eyes of their reason with the dust of desire.

CELESTINA. What is reason, you idiot? What is desire, you little donkey? You'll learn what they are only by using the discretion you do not yet possess. And wisdom is better than discretion; it comes only with experience, and experience only with age. We old ones are called parents, and good parents give good advice to their children, as I give you, whose life and honor are more precious to me than my own. And when will you repay me? Never! For parents and teachers cannot be paid with the same service.

PARMENO. I'm afraid, mother, that your advice is bad.

CELESTINA. So you refuse? Very well, I can only repeat what the wise one said, that that man who with a stiff neck scorns his teacher will come to a bad and sudden end, and health will not be in him. So, Parmeno, farewell to you and this business!

PARMENO. *My mother is angry and I'm doubtful of her advice. Still, as she says, it's an error to believe nothing and folly to believe everything. It's more human to have faith, especially in this one who promises both profit and love. I've heard that we should trust our elders. And, after all, what is her advice? To make peace with Sempronio. We shouldn't turn our back on peace, because blessed are the peacemakers, for they shall be called the children of God. Nor should we scorn love, for love and interest separate few brothers. I'll listen to her.* Mother, a teacher shouldn't get angry at the ignorance of the pupil, save occasionally for the sake of learning, which is by nature communicable, but which can be instilled in few places. So forgive me and speak, and I'll not only listen and believe, but will accept your advice as a rare gift. And don't thank me, for praise and thanks for an act should be rendered to the giver, not to the recipient. Therefore, command me and I'll obey you.

CELESTINA. Error is human and stubbornness is bestial. I'm pleased, therefore, my Parmeno, that you've wiped the thick cobwebs from your eyes and have lived up to the gratitude, discretion, and fine intelligence of your father, whose memory makes these old tears flow again. At times, like yourself, he'd cling to a foolish point, but in the end he always listened to reason. By God and my soul, seeing just now how stubborn you were and how you came round, I thought I saw him before me in the flesh! How handsome he was! How liberal! What a venerable face he had! But enough. Here come Calisto and your new friend Sempronio. Make your peace with him as soon as may be, for two people of a single mind are stronger than one, both for doing and understanding.

CALISTO. I've been so unlucky, mother, that I was doubting I should find you alive, and it's even more marvelous, so hot is my desire, that I'm alive myself! Receive this poor gift from one who offers you his life with it.

CELESTINA. Just as fine gold wrought by the hand of a master is of greater worth than the material, so do the grace and form of your sweet generosity make your magnificent gift more precious. A gift in time doubles its value, because one tardily given seems to deny the promise and show regret for the thing promised.

PARMENO. What did he give her, Sempronio?

SEMPRONIO. A hundred pieces of gold!

PARMENO. He, he, he!

SEMPRONIO. Did our mother speak with you?

PARMENO. She did indeed!

SEMPRONIO. Then how do we stand?

PARMENO. However you like, although I'm scared.

SEMPRONIO. Well, you'll be twice as scared before I'm done with you!

PARMENO. *My God! No pestilence is half so dangerous as an enemy in one's own house!*

CALISTO. Go now, mother, and cheer up your household, and then come back as quickly as you can and cheer up mine.

CELESTINA. God be with you!

CALISTO. And may He guard you for me!

ACT II

Calisto's house.   Calisto, Sempronio,
Parmeno.

CALISTO. Dear brothers, I gave our mother a hundred pieces of
gold. Did I do right?

SEMPRONIO. You did indeed! You not only found a remedy for
your trouble, but you did yourself great honor, because what is
good fortune for except to serve honor, which is the greatest of
worldly treasures? It's the prize and reward of virtue. That is
why we offer our honor to God, because it's the most precious
thing we've got. Honor is sullied by the heaping up of earthly
treasures, but magnificence and liberality win honor for you
and raise it to sublimity. Of what profit is it to get what is un-
profitable? I say that the spending of treasure is better than its
possession. What a glorious thing it is to give and how beggarly
it is to receive! As the act of giving is better than possession, so
is the giver more noble than the receiver. Fire is the noblest of
all the elements, for it is the most active, and thus it is given the
highest place among the spheres. Some say that that nobility is
the most praiseworthy which comes from the merit and antiquity of one's ancestors, but I say that reflected light will never
make you noble if you give off none of your own. Don't take too
much pride, therefore, in the nobility of your father, who indeed
was magnificent, but in your own, for thus you gain honor, which
is the highest good attainable by man. It follows that only a
good man like yourself is worthy of achieving perfect virtue, and
I say further that the attainment of virtue is not at odds with

honor. Rejoice, therefore, in your magnificence and liberality, and take my advice and go to bed, for your affair is in good hands. You may be sure that since it has begun so well it's bound to have a good ending. Let's go up now, for we have need to talk further.

CALISTO. It's not right, Sempronio, for me to stay here in pleasant company while she who is seeking my relief is out alone. Do you go with her and speed her on her way. Everything depends upon her diligence. If she loiters I shall suffer. I know you for a wise and faithful servant, so explain my malady to her and tell her how this fire is consuming me. Its heat is indeed so great that I wasn't able to describe the third part of my trouble to her, so tortured were my tongue and senses. You can speak freely to her; you're not sick.

SEMPRONIO. I want to obey you, but I think I ought to stay. I don't like this moodiness of yours. How can I leave you, seeing that as soon as I do you burst out raving like a madman, sighing, groaning, singing out of tune, avoiding company, and finding new ways to make yourself unhappy? If you go on like this you'll end up either as a lunatic or a corpse. You need someone to amuse you, to jest with you, to play gay airs, sing ballads and tell stories, to play cards or chess with you—in short, you need someone to take your mind off that unlucky first meeting with your lady.

CALISTO. You dolt! Don't you know that suffering is relieved by bewailing the cause of it? It's a sweet thing for the sad to be able to mourn. There's consolation in sighing, and pain is greatly lessened by groans and tears. All the authorities agree in this.

SEMPRONIO. You should have read further and turned the page, and you'd have learned that to look for excuses to make yourself miserable is a kind of madness. Don't kick against the pricks. Make believe you're happy and easy in your mind, and so you will be, for belief, although it doesn't change the nature of things, will often make them seem to be as we wish, and will moderate our grief and restore our judgment.

CALISTO. Since you're so reluctant to leave me alone, Sempronio, you may call Parmeno and he'll stay with me. Be faithful to me as is your habit, for the faithfulness of the servant is the reward of the master.

PARMENO. I'm here, sir!

CALISTO. But I'm not, for I didn't even see you! . . . . Sempronio, don't leave her or neglect my affair, and God go with you! . . . . Parmeno, what do you think of what happened today? I'm in great pain, Melibea is out of reach, and Celestina is a wise and good physician for this kind of disease. We must not fail. Your hatred of her is so violent that you've confirmed my belief in her, for truth is strong and will win out over its enemies. So then, allowing that Celestina is such a person as you say, I'd rather give a hundred pieces of gold to her than five to another.

PARMENO. *Weeping already? Here's a state of things! We'll have to pay for your extravagance!*

CALISTO. Be kind to me, Parmeno. I'm only asking you to tell me what you think. And don't cast your eyes down when you answer. Envy is a sad thing and sadness is silent. Your envy of Celestina is stronger than your fear of me. . . . What were you saying just now, you unmannerly rascal?

PARMENO. I was saying, sir, that your liberality would be better employed in buying gifts for Melibea than in giving money to this old crone I know so well. And what is worse, you've made yourself her captive.

CALISTO. What do you mean, you ass, her captive?

PARMENO. You give up your liberty when you entrust your secrets to another.

CALISTO. There's something in what the fool says! But I say that when there's a great distance between the seeker and the sought, either in rank or wealth, or when one of them scorns the other, as Melibea does me, I need someone to get my message to her, although I doubt I'll ever see her again. Such being the case, tell me if you approve of my action.

PARMENO. *Let the devil approve of it!*

CALISTO. What did you say?

PARMENO. I said, sir, that evils never come singly and that one misfortune opens the door for many more.

CALISTO. I like what you say, but I don't understand your reason for saying it.

PARMENO. Sir, you lost your falcon the other day, and that was why you entered Melibea's garden to look for it; getting into her garden was the occasion for your seeing her and speaking with her; that led to love; love caused your pain; and pain lost you your body, your soul, and your money. But what I most regret is that you fell into the clutches of that old go-between who has been given three coats of feathers already for plying her trade.

CALISTO. Don't stop, Parmeno! The more you speak against her the better I like it! So long as she does her duty by me let her wear a fourth coat! You're unfeeling, Parmeno! My suffering means nothing to you.

PARMENO. It's better to have you angry with me now for speaking out than to have you curse me later for keeping silent. You lost the name of free man when you sold yourself into captivity.

CALISTO. This rascal's asking for a beating! Tell me, oaf, why do you speak so ill of her? What do you know about honor? What is love, do you think? Where are your manners? How can you set yourself up to preach at me? Don't you know that the first step in folly is to think yourself wise? You don't really feel my pain, or you'd wash my wound with a gentler lotion. Sempronio brings me medicine and you spoil it with your sharp tongue. You pretend to be loyal to me, but you're nothing but a lump of flattery, a sack of malice, the very hearth and dwelling place of envy! Just to defame an old woman by fair means or foul, you'd sow distrust of her in me? You drive me frantic! Sempronio didn't want to leave you here with me, but I told him to go and now I'm sorry I did. Better alone than in bad company!

PARMENO. Sir, it would be a poor kind of loyalty that fear of punishment would turn to flattery, especially with a master who's out of his senses with love. But one day your eyes will be opened and you'll see that my harsh words were a better cure for your sickness than Sempronio's soft ones, which only fan your flame and make it burn the hotter, and add fuel to it until it will go out only with your own death!

CALISTO. Enough, you paltry wretch! I in misery and you babbling platitudes? Well, I expected nothing else from you! Have my horse brought out and see that he's well groomed and cinched. By chance I may pass the house of my mistress and my goddess!

PARMENO. Boy! Isn't there a groom in the house? I'll have to do it myself. Well, from now on I'll be doing worse things than playing stable boy. Come! Get on with you! Tell the truth and see how you get paid for it! Are you whinnying, sir horse? Isn't one beast in heat enough for one house? Or do you smell Melibea?

CALISTO. Where's my horse? What are you doing out there, Parmeno?

PARMENO. Here it is, sir. Sosia's away.

CALISTO. Hold my stirrup and open the door wider. If Sempronio returns with the old mistress tell him to wait. I'll soon be back.

PARMENO. May you never come back! The devil is in him! Try and get these lunatics to listen to what's good for them! They won't even look at you! Poor fool that I was! It's what I get for being loyal, while others profit by their treachery. That's the way the world wags! But from now on I'll swim with the current, since traitors are called wise, and the loyal, fools! If I throw in with Celestina, with her six dozens of years to her back, Calisto will like it. I've learned my lesson! From now on, if he says, "Let's eat," I'll do the same. If he wants to pull down the house, I'll lend a hand. If he takes a notion to burn up his estate, I'll run for the tinderbox. Let him destroy, break, smash, spoil, and give his money to go-betweens! I'll get my share! I'll fish in troubled waters! I'll not be caught again!

ACT III

SCENE 1. *A street. Sempronio, Celestina.*

SEMPRONIO. How poky the old thing is! Her feet were a little livelier on her way here! That's what happens when you pay in advance! Ho there, Celestina! You're certainly taking your time!

CELESTINA. What is it, my son?

SEMPRONIO. Our patient doesn't know what he wants. He isn't satisfied; he's on pins and needles. He's afraid you'll neglect this affair of his and he's cursing himself for his stinginess, he gave you so little.

CELESTINA. We must expect lovers to be impatient. Every delay is torture. They want to see all their schemes realized instantly, completed before they're begun, especially these novices in love who rise to every bait without thinking they may be doing harm to themselves or their servants.

SEMPRONIO. What's that about servants? Are you saying that we may come to grief in this business and get ourselves scorched by Calisto's fire? To the devil with him! At the first sign of a hitch I'll back out. I'd rather lose the wages he owes me than my life in trying to collect them. I'll know what to do when the time comes. Before he collapses he'll give some warning, like a falling house. I think, mother, we'd better keep out of danger, whatever happens, now or later. Nothing is so hard to bear at the beginning that it isn't softened and made more tolerable with time. No wound is so painful that time doesn't lessen its sting. No pleasure is so great that time doesn't reduce it. Good and evil, prosperity and adversity, glory and pain—everything loses its first vigor with time. We see wonderful things happen, we hear them and take part in them, and then leave them behind us. Time reduces them and makes them relative. It would be an astonishing thing if you heard there had been an earthquake, or some such matter, and didn't forget it at once. As, for example: the river is frozen over; the blind man has recovered his sight; your father is dead; a thunderbolt has struck; Granada has fallen; the king is coming today; the Turk has been defeated; there will be an eclipse tomorrow; the bridge is washed out; So-and-so has been made a bishop; Peter got robbed; Inez has been hanged. And so forth. That's what will happen with this love of my master's: the longer it lasts the less it will amount to. So we'd better strike while the iron is hot. And if we can keep out of trouble at the same time, that will be still better. We might try to bring Melibea round. If we can't do one thing or the other, well, it's better for the master to suffer than for the servant to risk his skin.

CELESTINA. Good! I'm with you. We can't go wrong. Still, my son, a good lawyer must do a little work now and then: look up a few false arguments or citations and attend court, even if the judge scolds him. He wouldn't want it said of him that he does nothing to earn his money. In that way everyone will go to him for legal advice and to Celestina with their love business.

SEMPRONIO. Do as you think best. This is not the first affair of this kind you've managed, I'll wager.

CELESTINA. The first, my son? You haven't seen many virgins set up shop in this town, praise God!, whose goods I haven't been the first to peddle. When a girl baby is born I write her name down in my book just to keep track of how many get away from me. What did you think, Sempronio, that I was going to live on air? What have I got but my profession? Did I inherit any estate but this? Have I got any other means of support? Any other house or vineyard? How did you think I earned my food and drink? Or dressed and shod myself? Born in this city, raised here, holding my head up with the best of them, am I not famous then? Whoever doesn't know my name and address, consider him a stranger!

SEMPRONIO. What did you tell Parmeno, mother, when I went up with Calisto to get your money?

CELESTINA. Everything! I told him he had more to gain by coming along with us than by flattering his master; that unless he changed his ways he'd always be poor and despised; and that he shouldn't try to play the saint with an old dog like me. And I reminded him of who his mother was so he wouldn't take a high moral tone about my trade and would stumble over her if he tried to talk me down.

SEMPRONIO. Have you known him so long, mother?

CELESTINA. This Celestina saw him born and helped to raise him. His mother and I were thick as thieves. She taught me whatever I know. We ate together, slept together, and together took our pleasures and did our business. Indoors and out we were like two sisters. I never earned a penny but I shared it with her. If only she had lived I shouldn't have been cheated as I have been. How many good friends does death take from us! For every one it takes after a long life it cuts off a thousand while they're young. If she had lived I shouldn't be friendless and alone. May she rest in peace, for she was a loyal companion and a good friend to me! If her son were like her his master wouldn't have a rag left by this time, nor should we have anything to complain of. But I'll bring him round if I live! I'll make him one of us!

SEMPRONIO. Do you think you can do it? He's a traitor!

CELESTINA. It takes a thief to catch a thief. I'll get him tangled up with Areusa, and then he'll belong to us and help us spread the net to catch Calisto's gold.

SEMPRONIO. What can you do with Melibea? Have you got some kind of hold on her?

CELESTINA. No surgeon can diagnose a wound at the first probe. I'll tell you what I know: Melibea is beautiful; Calisto is mad and open-handed. It won't hurt him to spend or me to trot. So long as he jingles his money his suit can last as long as it wants. Money is what does the trick: it can level mountains and cross the rivers dryshod. There's no peak so high that an ass loaded with gold can't climb it. Calisto is crazy enough to ruin himself and make our fortunes. That's all I've smelled out so far. No matter how fierce Melibea may prove to be, she's not the first one, please God!, that I've made to stop her cackling. They're all skittish in the beginning, but once they feel the saddle on their back they turn gentle soon enough. They've got the course to themselves and they'll run till they drop. They never get tired. If they run by night they never want the sun to rise; they curse the clock because it goes so fast, and the cocks because they announce the day. That's the road, my son, that I never wearied of traveling! I couldn't get enough! Old as I am, God knows I'd like to take to that same road again! And if that's true for me, how much truer it is for these fillies whose blood is racing in their veins! They yield at the first embrace; they beg those who begged them; they suffer with the suffering; they become the slaves of their former slaves; they give over commanding and are commanded; they open windows; they pretend illness; they oil the squeaking hinges of their doors. I can't tell you how sweet in their mouth is the taste of their first kisses! They fly the means and perch themselves on the extremes.

SEMPRONIO. What do you mean by that, mother?

CELESTINA. I mean that a woman either loves the man who pursues her, or she hates him, one thing or the other. I know this so well that I'm going to Melibea's house as confidently as if I held her in my hand. I'll have to plead with her at first, but in the end she'll be pleading with me. She'll threaten me at the beginning, but flatter me in the end. As a pretext for getting into houses where they don't know me I carry a bit of thread in my bag, along with other trifles, such as ruffs, hair nets, fringes, tweezers, mascara, whiting, and even needles and pins, something for every occasion, so that wherever I'm called I can bait my traps and get about my business without wasting time.

SEMPRONIO. Mother, you'd better be sure of what you're doing. If you take a false step now it will go hard with you later. Think of her father, noble and powerful, and her mother, jealous and stern, and yourself, who are suspicion in person. Melibea is all they've got; if they lose her they lose everything. It scares me to think of it. Don't go to market for wool and lose your own feathers.

CELESTINA. Feathers, my son?

SEMPRONIO. Or get another coat of them, which will be worse.

CELESTINA. Upon my word I picked out a fine companion! As if you could give Celestina lessons in her profession! Why, I cut my eye teeth before you were born! What a big help you are, you sack of fears and bad luck!

SEMPRONIO. Don't blame me, mother. It's only natural to doubt that what you want so badly will ever happen. In this case I'm afraid that you and I may have to pay too dearly. I want to make money and I'd like to see this affair turn out well, not so much to help my master, but to get out of this poverty I'm in. That's the way I see things; but, then, I haven't had as much experience in this kind of business as you've had.

SCENE 2.   *Celestina's house.   Celestina, Sempronio, Elicia.*

ELICIA. Sempronio! A miracle! Knock me down with a feather! Twice in the same day?

CELESTINA. Shut up, you fool! Don't tease him. We've got more important things on our minds. Tell me, is there anyone in the house? Did that girl go who was waiting for the friar?

ELICIA. Yes, and there's been another one since.

CELESTINA. So? Did she get what she wanted?

ELICIA. God forbid! The early bird may get the worm, but the one that's got God on its side does even better.

CELESTINA. Well, go up to the garret and bring me down the bottle of snake oil you'll find hanging by the piece of rope I got that rainy night at the crossroads. And open the yarn box and you'll find at the far end a vial of bat's blood. It's under the wing of that dragon whose claws we drew yesterday. And mind you don't spill the May-water I'm making on order.

ELICIA. Mother, it isn't where you say. You never remember where you put things!

CELESTINA. For God's sake don't try to reform me in my old age! Don't scold me, Elicia. Don't put on a show just because Sempronio's here listening to you. And don't get so high and mighty, for he'd rather have me for a counsellor any day than you for a mistress, no matter how much you love him. Go look in the closet where I keep the ointments and you'll find it in the black cat's skin where I told you to put the eyes of that bitch wolf. And bring down at the same time the blood of that he-goat and some of his whiskers that you cut off for me.

ELICIA. Here it all is, mother. I'm going upstairs now with Sempronio.

CELESTINA. Sad Pluto, lord of the underworld, emperor of the court of the damned, proud captain of the fallen angels, master of the sulphureous fires that gush from boiling Etna, governor and inspector of the torments and the tormentors of the souls in hell, I, Celestina, thy most renowned client, conjure thee by these red letters I write in the blood of the bat, by the power of the words and signs herein contained, and by the sharp poison of the vipers with whose oil I anoint this thread, to come forthwith obedient to my call and so wrap thyself in it that thou delay not an instant till Melibea opportunely buy it and be so caught and entangled in it that her heart will be softened to grant my petition. And lay thou her heart open and so strike her with the strong and cruel love of Calisto that, forsaking all modesty, she will bare herself to me and reward me for my effort and my message. When thou hast done this, ask of me what thou wilt. But if thou do it not, and quickly, thou shalt have me for thy mortal enemy; I shall strike thy dark and gloomy dungeons with light, make public thine endless lies, and cover thy horrid name with curses! Again and yet again I conjure thee, trusting in my great power, and thus I depart with my thread, in which I have thee now enwrapped, *or so I think.*

ACT IV

SCENE 1. *A street. Celestina.*

CELESTINA. Now that I'm alone let's take a closer look at what Sempronio said, for things that aren't properly thought out ahead of time, even though they may turn out well, usually produce ill effects, just as forethought always yields good ones. I wasn't quite frank with him, to be sure, and it could well be that if my designs on Melibea are discovered I'll pay heavily for it, possibly with my life. And even if they don't kill me they'll toss me in a blanket or whip me. In that event my hundred pieces of gold will be bitterly earned indeed! What a trap I've got myself into! Just to prove how clever and strong I am, I stake my life on a cast of the dice! What shall I do, fool that I am? I can't back out without loss and I can't go on without danger. Which shall it be? Where does the ox go that he doesn't drag the plow? There's no road without potholes. If I get caught with the plunder the least I can expect is to get killed or exposed in the stocks. This is what my hard work, my knowledge and skill, my cleverness and promises, have brought me to!

What will Calisto say? What will he do? What will he think, save that I've lied to him and revealed his plan in order to get money from the other side? And even if that ugly thought doesn't occur to him he'll scream like a madman and shout insults in my face and tax me with obstructing him in a thousand ways. "You old whore! Why did you encourage me with your promises? You false bawd! You've got feet for everyone else, for me only a tongue; for others deeds, for me, words; for others, toil, for me, nothing; for everyone else, light, for me, darkness!

Why then, old traitor, did you offer to help me? You gave me hope and hope kept me alive, delayed my death, made me a happy man. And now it has all come to nothing, and I shall die in despair and you in agony!" What a fix to be in! Evil here and evil there, trouble no matter where I turn! Well, if I must choose between extremes it's better to choose the healthier. It will be safer to offend Pleberio than to anger Calisto. I'll go. Better to keep my word and suffer for it than to face the shame of backing out from cowardice. Fortune never failed to aid the bold.

But here's her door. I've been in tighter spots. Courage, Celestina! Don't falter! You can always find a lawyer to get you off the worst of it. All the omens are favorable, or I know nothing of the art. Of the four men I passed, three were named John and two were cuckolds. The first word I heard in the street was of love. I didn't stumble as I have at other times. Not a single dog barked at me, nor did I see a raven or crow or any other night bird. And, best of all, there's Lucrecia at Melibea's door. She's Elicia's cousin and won't get in the way.

SCENE 2.   *Pleberio's house.   Lucrecia,*
Celestina.   Alisa, Melibea.

LUCRECIA. I wonder who the old woman is, scurrying this way.

CELESTINA. Peace be in this house!

LUCRECIA. Celestina! Welcome, dear mother! What lucky wind blew you out of your ordinary course?

CELESTINA. Love, my daughter, and my desire to see you and bring you word of Elicia, and also to see your two mistresses, whom I haven't laid eyes on since I moved to the other side of town.

LUCRECIA. Is that your only reason? You amaze me! It's not your habit to step out unless there's money in it.

CELESTINA. What greater profit is there, silly, than for a person to do what she likes? Besides, since we old ones are always in need, especially myself who have to support other people's daughters, I brought some thread to sell.

LUCRECIA. I said it! I haven't lost my wits. You never poke in your finger but you come up with a whole pie! It just happens that my mistress is weaving a piece of goods and needs some thread. So come in and wait and you won't lose by it.

ALISA. Who's there, Lucrecia?

LUCRECIA. That old woman, mistress, with the scar on her face who used to live down near the tanneries.

ALISA. That doesn't mean anything to me. You'll have to speak more plainly.

LUCRECIA. Goodness, mistress, everybody knows her! Surely you remember that time she was exposed in the stocks for a witch and for selling her girls to priests and ruining a thousand matrons?

ALISA. What does she do now? Perhaps I'll know her by her trade.

LUCRECIA. Mistress, she's a perfumer, she makes whiting, and has thirty other trades. She sells herbs and doctors babies, and some say she deals in magic stones.

ALISA. I still don't know her. Tell me her name, if you know it.

LUCRECIA. Do I know it! There's no one in the whole city, young or old, who doesn't!

ALISA. Well, come out with it!

LUCRECIA. I'm ashamed to.

ALISA. Don't be a fool! Tell me. Do you want me to lose my temper?

LUCRECIA. Her name, mistress, speaking with due reverence, is Celestina.

ALISA. He, he, he! Plague take you! I can't help laughing. How you must hate the old crone! I'm beginning to remember her. A pretty piece of goods! But that's enough. She must want something. Tell her to come up.

LUCRECIA. Come up, aunt.

CELESTINA. Dear lady, may the grace of God be with you and your noble daughter! I've been too sick and troubled to visit you as I should, but God knows my good intentions. Distance cannot dim the love in my heart, and now my necessity has brought me to see you. Among my many misfortunes I'm in need of money, so I've come to sell some thread I'd been saving to make veils with. Poor as it is, it's at your service, as I am.

ALISA. Honest neighbor, your words and your offer so affect me that I'd like to help you instead of taking your thread. I'm grateful for your kind thoughts. If your thread is as you say I'll give you a good price for it.

CELESTINA. It's as excellent, my lady, as I hope my old age will be! Fine as hair, strong as a fiddle string, white as snow, all spun and reeled by these fingers! Take this skein. Yesterday, on my soul as a sinner, I got three pence an ounce for it!

ALISA. Daughter Melibea, do you stay with this honest woman. I've got to visit my sister who's been taken worse. I haven't seen her since yesterday and she sent her page to call me.

CELESTINA. *The devil's about! He's made the sister worse just to give me an opening!*

ALISA. What are you saying there, my friend?

CELESTINA. I was saying, my lady, that your sister's illness is the devil's doing and we sha'n't be able to finish our business. What ails your sister?

ALISA. She came down with a pleurisy, and it's so bad that I'm afraid it will be the death of her. In your prayers, neighbor, ask God to give her health.

CELESTINA. I promise you, my lady, I'll go directly by the monastery, where I've got some good friends, and give them your message, and I'll tell my beads for her four times before breakfast.

ALISA. Melibea, do you give our neighbor a fair price for her thread. And please forgive me, mother. We'll see each other again.

CELESTINA. Where there's no fault, my lady, there can be no forgiveness. God bless you! You leave me in good company! . . . . And may God grant, my lady Melibea, that you enjoy your noble youth while it's in flower, which is the time of most pleasure and the greatest delight! Upon my word, old age is nothing but an inn of infirmities, the abode of melancholy and abominations, a never-ending vexation, an incurable sore, regret for things past, pain in the present, and worry for the future, a near neighbor of death, a badly thatched hut that lets in the rain from all directions, a flimsy staff that bends under the slightest weight!

MELIBEA. Why, mother, do you speak so ill of what everyone so ardently desires to see?

CELESTINA. They desire much evil for themselves and great trouble. They would reach the end of their journey because they're living while they're on the way, and living is sweet, and by living they grow old. Thus the child would be a youth, the youth an old man, and the old man older yet, with all his infirmities. All this merely to live! As they say, let the hen live, even if she's got the pip! But, lady, who could tell you all its afflictions, its troubles, its fatigues, its ailments, its heat, its cold, its discontent, its dejections, that wrinkling of the face, that changing of the hair as it loses its first freshness, that deafness, that weak sight and that retreating of the eyes into their sockets, that sinking of the cheeks, that falling out of the teeth, that slow eating! Alas, alas, my lady! And worst of all, if old age is accompanied by poverty, all else is as nothing! To have a good appetite and nothing to eat! I've never felt a worse stomach ache than hunger!

MELIBEA. Each man speaks of the race according to his stake in it. The rich would probably sing a different tune.

CELESTINA. My lady, my daughter, every road has its three leagues of bad going. The rich lose their pleasure, their renown, and their ease down a different drain, which is bricked over and hidden by flattery. Every rich man has a dozen children and grandchildren whose single prayer is to have him removed from among them. They can hardly wait to see the moment when they'll have him safely underground and his wealth in their hands, and at little cost they can lay him in his last resting place.

MELIBEA. Mother, if that is so, you must greatly regret the youth you've lost. Wouldn't you like to return to it?

CELESTINA. A fool is that traveler, my lady, who, wearied by the hardships of his journey, would undertake it anew, merely to arrive once again at the very place where he now is. It is better to have suffered hardships than to have them still before you, because the farther you have fared from their beginning, the nearer you are to their end. There's no sweeter sight to the weary traveler than the inn where he may rest. Therefore, though youth be a pleasant time, your true ancient doesn't desire it, for he lacks both wit and sense who desires only what he has lost.

MELIBEA. If only to live longer, I still say it's good to be young.

CELESTINA. The lamb, my lady, goes as soon to the slaughter as the sheep. No one's so old that he can't live another year, nor so young that he can't die today. You've got little advantage of us in that.

MELIBEA. You amaze me, mother. Your words make me think I've seen you before. Tell me, aren't you Celestina, she who used to live by the tanneries near the river?

CELESTINA. Your servant, my lady!

MELIBEA. You're old! They say truly that our days don't pass without taking their toll. Upon my word, I shouldn't have known you except by that scar on your face! I imagine you once were beautiful, but you seem like a different person, you're so changed!

LUCRECIA. *He, he, he! The devil's changed! With that scar half across her face!*

MELIBEA. What are you saying, fool? Why are you laughing?

LUCRECIA. I'm laughing because you didn't recognize her, although it's been such a short time since you saw her.

MELIBEA. Two years isn't such a short time, and then her face has got so wrinkled!

CELESTINA. My lady, do you stop the passing of time and I'll stop my face from wrinkling! A day will come when you'll not know yourself in the glass. Besides, I turned gray very young and look twice my age. By my soul as a sinner, of the four daughters my mother bore, I was the youngest! So you see I'm not as old as they say!

MELIBEA. Well, friend Celestina, I'm very happy to have made your acquaintance and I've enjoyed talking with you. Take your money now and go with God, for I imagine you haven't eaten.

CELESTINA. Oh my lovely angel, my precious pearl, and how sweetly you speak! What a joy to hear you! But don't you know what God said to the tempter, that we don't live by bread alone? And so it is: we aren't sustained merely by eating, especially myself, for sometimes I fast for one or two days while I'm about my neighbors' business, working for good people to the limit of my strength, for I've always worked for others rather than for my own pleasure. So with your permission I'll tell you the urgent reason for my visit. It's so urgent, indeed, that we'd both regret it if I left without telling you what it is.

MELIBEA. Tell me your needs, mother, and if I can help you I'll do so very gladly. It's my duty to a neighbor and an old friend.

CELESTINA. *My* needs, my lady? Not mine, but another's, for I keep mine at home out of sight, eating when I can and drinking when I've got something to drink. Although I'm poor, since I became a widow I've never lacked, thank God!, a penny for bread and a farthing for wine. Before then I lived in plenty: a full wineskin always in the house and another one empty. I never went to bed without my dish of crusts soaked in wine and a couple of dozen sips after each bite for my stomach's sake; but now that I must look after myself they bring me only one leaky little jug of it that holds hardly half a gallon. A house without a man is a house lacking all good things. The spindle turns badly when there's no man behind it. I say all this, my lady, to explain what I meant about the needs of others, not my own.

MELIBEA. Ask what you wish, it doesn't matter for whom.

CELESTINA. Gracious and high-born lady, your gentle words and sweet face, and your generosity toward this poor old woman, give me courage to speak. I come from one who is sick unto death, from one who with a single word from your noble lips, which I shall bring him hidden in my breast, believes he'll be cured, so greatly does he prize your courtesy.

MELIBEA. Honest old woman, unless you speak more clearly I'll not know what you're talking about. On the one hand you annoy me and arouse my anger; on the other you move me to pity. I can't give you a proper answer, I understand you so little. I'll be happy if the well-being of any Christian depends only upon my word, for to do good to one's fellows is to resemble God, and he who does good to a worthy person shall be rewarded. Besides, they say that a person who can heal the sick man and fails to do so, kills him. So don't hold back from shyness or fear.

CELESTINA. I lost my fear, my lady, when I saw how beautiful you are. I can't believe that God made some faces more perfect than others, and endowed them with more graces and lovely features, except to make them a storehouse of virtue, compassion, and mercy, ministers of His bounty, as He made yours. Since we're all mortal, born only to die, he can't be said to have been born who lives only for himself, but would resemble the beasts. And even among them there are merciful ones, as it is said of the unicorn, who kneels before any virgin. And the birds? The cock eats nothing but he calls his hens to share it with him. Why should we be less pitiful than they? Why not share our blessings with our neighbors, especially with one who is sick of a secret malady, such a strange disease, indeed, that it can be cured only by what caused it.

MELIBEA. Good Lord! Without further beating about the bush tell me who is this sick man and what is this complicated malady of his!

CELESTINA. You must have heard, my lady, of a noble young gentleman of this city whose name is Calisto?

MELIBEA. Aha, my good woman! So this is the patient who inspires your arguments! Go no further! So he is the one who induced you to come here and get yourself killed? So he is the one for whom you have taken these dangerous steps, you shameless and bearded old hag? What ails this scoundrel that you should plead for him so passionately? He must be sick in the head! What were you thinking of? If you had found me off my guard with that maniac, what words you would have used to wheedle me! It's a true saying that the most harmful part of a wicked man or woman is the tongue! You're going to burn for this, you false procuress! Sweet Jesus! Lucrecia, take her away! I can't stand this! I'm going to swoon! But I deserve it and worse for listening to such a bawd! The only reason I don't put an end to you and your mission at once is that I've got some regard for my reputation and don't want to publish the insolence of that villain!

CELESTINA. *I came here in an evil hour if my incantation has failed. Ho there! I know to whom I speak!*

MELIBEA. Muttering in my presence? Just to double my anger and your punishment? You would ruin me to save the life of a lunatic? And make money out of my ruin? And destroy the house and honor of my father for the profit of an accursed old woman? Do you imagine I don't know what you're up to with your abominable message? Well, I'll warrant you that your punishment will be such that you'll no longer be an offense to God! Answer me, traitor! How dared you?

CELESTINA. Fear ties my tongue. My innocence gives me courage, but the sight of your angry face silences me. What hurts me most is to be accused unjustly. Please, dear lady, hear me out and you'll see that he is not to be blamed, nor I condemned, for it was all done in the service of God, not dishonesty. If I'd thought, dear lady, that you'd jump so hastily to conclusions, your permission wouldn't have been enough to make me talk about Calisto or any man.

MELIBEA. Don't mention the name of that fool, that wall-climber, that nighthawk, skinny as a stork, with a face like a badly daubed signboard! And if that isn't true may I drop dead this minute! He's the one who saw me yesterday and began raving at me and playing the gallant! Tell him, good old woman, that if he thought he'd won the field just because I listened to his idiocies, it was because I let him go for a maniac rather than punish him and make public his folly! And tell him to give over trying to see me and it will be the better for him. Otherwise, he may find that he never paid so dearly for an interview in his life! These madmen always think everyone else is mad. Take that answer to him and don't expect any other. And give thanks to God that you're getting off so easily! I'd been warned about you and your tricks. I let you in because I didn't recognize you at first.

CELESTINA. *Troy was stronger, and I've tamed fiercer ones than you! No tempest lasts for long.*

MELIBEA. What are you mumbling there, you wretch? Speak up! Have you any excuse for your audacity?

CELESTINA. So long as you're angry with me my excuses will only do me harm. You're harsh, and I'm not surprised, for young blood boils at a low heat.

MELIBEA. Low? Low indeed, since you've escaped with your life and I'm angry only at your impudence! What can you say in that fellow's defence that would please me? You say I didn't let you finish your speech. Well, finish it then, unless you want to pay for what you've already done!

CELESTINA. All he wants, my lady, is a certain prayer to St. Apolonia for the toothache they say you know, and your silken girdle which it is believed has touched all the relics in Rome and Jerusalem. This was my message, but, since you got so angry with me, let him suffer with his toothache for having chosen such an unlucky messenger!

MELIBEA. Well, if that was all you wanted, why didn't you say so in the first place? And then you came out with it so abruptly!

CELESTINA. My lady, I was so innocent that I thought you'd not suspect me of evil intentions, no matter how briefly I might speak. If I didn't explain myself at greater length it was because truth doesn't have to be painted in many colors. My pity for Calisto's suffering and my trust in your generosity made me curtail my suit. You know, my lady, that anxiety makes one's tongue clumsy, so please forgive me. If he was in error don't punish me for it. My only mistake was to act as messenger. Don't be like the spiderweb that uses its strength only against the weak. Don't make the righteous pay for the sinner, for divine justice decrees that only the soul that sins shall die, and human justice says never to condemn the father for the sins of the child, nor the child for the sins of the father. Nor is it just, my lady, that Calisto's insolence should be made the cause of my ruin.

My profession is to serve my fellows: I make my living and clothe myself by it. I never harm some in order to please others, whatever you may have heard to the contrary. In short, my lady, the wind of gossip cannot hurt the truth.

MELIBEA. I've heard such tales of your wiles that I can't believe you even when you merely ask me for a prayer!

CELESTINE. May I never pray again, or may my prayers never be heard, if I say anything different, even if they put me on the rack!

MELIBEA. I'm still too angry to laugh at your excuse as I should. I know that neither oath nor torture could ever twist the truth out of you because you're incapable of it!

CELESTINA. You are my lady mistress. I must hold my tongue. I must serve you and you must command me. You're scolding me today, but tomorrow you'll give me a new skirt.

MELIBEA. You'll certainly have earned it!

CELESTINA. I may not have earned it with my tongue, but neither will I have lost it through bad intentions.

MELIBEA. You so insist upon your innocence that you almost make me believe you're telling the truth, so I'll suspend judgment and not refuse your request because of my hasty interpretation of it. Don't be astonished at my outburst, for there were two things in your speech, either one of which was enough to make me lose my temper. First, you named that gentleman who dared speak to me, and second, you sought me out for no good reason and I could only suspect something damaging to my honor. But, since everything was well meant, I'll forgive him. My heart is somewhat lightened thereby, for it's a holy and pious thing to heal the suffering and the sick.

CELESTINA. And what a patient he is, my lady! If you only knew him you'd think differently of him. By God and my soul, he's all sweetness! He's got a thousand graces: in liberality, an Alexander; in bravery, a Hector! His countenance is that of a king!

He's witty and merry, and melancholy is not in him! He's of noble blood, as you know, a great jouster, and when he's dressed in armor he looks a veritable St. George! Hercules himself had no such strength! I'd need a new tongue to describe his presence, his features, his symmetry, his grace! He's altogether like an angel from heaven! I swear that the noble Narcissus, he who fell in love with his own reflection, was not so beautiful! And to think, my lady, that he's been brought low by a toothache!

MELIBEA. How long has he had it?

CELESTINA. He's about twenty-three, my lady, as I well know, for I saw him born and delivered him.

MELIBEA. I didn't ask you that, nor do I want to know his age, but only how long has he been suffering with his tooth?

CELESTINA. A week, my lady, although it seems like a year to judge by his altered appearance. His only relief is to take up his lute and sing the mournfullest songs, sadder, I think, than those which the great musician-emperor Hadrian sang when he felt his death approaching. I know little of music, but it seems to me he makes his lute talk. The very birds stop to listen when he sings, with more pleasure than they listened to Orpheus of old, whose fame wouldn't be so great if Calisto had been living then. Therefore, my lady, consider how happy a poor old woman like me would be if she could restore the life of one so gifted! No woman sees him but gives thanks to God who made him! And if by chance she speaks with him she's no longer her own mistress, but must do what he wishes. I'm so right about him, my lady, that you must judge my purpose to be good, my efforts wholesome, and me free of suspicion of wrong.

MELIBEA. How sorry I am that I lost my temper! He in his ignorance and you in your innocence have suffered from my angry tongue, although, to be sure, I had some reason to suspect you. Well, to repay you for your patience with me I'll grant your request and give you my girdle. If that's not enough, come tomorrow very secretly and get the prayer, for there isn't time to write it down now before my mother returns.

LUCRECIA. *Oho! My mistress is undone! So she wants Celestina to come secretly? There's trouble brewing! She'll give her more than she thinks!*

MELIBEA. What are you saying there, Lucrecia?

LUCRECIA. I was saying, mistress, that we've talked enough, for it's getting late.

MELIBEA. Now, mother, don't tell that gentleman everything that happened. I wouldn't want him to think me cruel or hasty or forward.

LUCRECIA. *I was right! This business will come to no good!*

CELESTINA. I'm much surprised, my lady, that you should doubt my ability to keep a secret. Don't be afraid; I can hide anything. I'll take your girdle and go my way happily. I can hear him thanking you in his heart, and I see him improved already.

MELIBEA. I'll do more for your patient, if necessary, to alleviate his suffering.

CELESTINA. *You'll do more than that, even though you get no thanks for it!*

MELIBEA. What did you say about thanks, mother?

CELESTINA. I was saying, my lady, that we're all thankful and that we'll all serve you and be in your debt. *Payment is certain when one holds the proper security!*

LUCRECIA. Change those words around, mother!

CELESTINA. Hush, daughter! Come to my house and I'll give you a rinse for your hair that will turn it brighter than gold. And I'll give you some powders for that bad breath of yours—no one in the whole kingdom can make them as I do—for bad breath is the worst thing a woman can have the matter with her.

MELIBEA. What were you saying to Lucrecia, mother?

CELESTINA. Just something between us, my lady.

MELIBEA. Tell me! It's very provoking to have people talk in my presence and leave me out of it.

CELESTINA. My lady, I told her to remind you of the prayer and that you should have her write it down. And I told her to be patient with you, as I have been, while you are vexed. As the proverb has it: leave the angry one alone for a short time, your enemy forever. You, my lady, were angry at what you suspected in my words; you were not my enemy. But even if my words had been as you thought, they were not evil in themselves, for every day you'll see men desiring women, and women, men. Thus nature works as God ordained, and God did nothing evil. And thus my petition, whatever else it may have been, was praiseworthy in itself, since it had such a source, and I was blameless. I could speak at length about this matter, only long-windedness is tedious to the hearer and does the speaker no good.

MELIBEA. You've been wise in everything: in keeping silent while I was angry, and in your great patience with me.

CELESTINA. My lady, it was fear that made me patient, because you were justly angry, and anger backed by power is a thunderbolt. That's why I suffered your cruel words in silence until you had exhausted your magazine.

MELIBEA. That gentleman is in your debt.

CELESTINA. He deserves even more, my lady. I've got something for him with my pleading, but I've hurt him by being so long about it. So now, with your permission, I'll go to him.

MELIBEA. If you'd asked my permission sooner I'd have given it more readily. Go with God! Your message has brought me no profit and no harm can come to me from your going.

ACT V

SCENE 1. *A street. Celestina, Sempronio.*

CELESTINA. What a scrape I was in! How bold I was! How patient! And how close to death, if I hadn't been cunning enough to run to cover in time! How ferocious she was! Oh my good devil, how well you kept your word! I'm obliged to you! You tamed that rampaging female and got her mother out of the way so I could talk as much as I wished! Old Celestina, are you happy? Well begun is half done! Oh my snake oil and my white thread, how well you did your part! If you hadn't, I'd break up all my charms and no longer put my trust in herbs or stones or incantations. Cheer up, old woman! You'll get more out of this business than out of fifteen patched maidenheads! Damn these long skirts! How they get in my way! Fortune always favors the bold and defeats the timid. The coward can't escape death by running away. How many others would have missed where I hit the mark! What would these novices in my profession have done if they'd found themselves in such a tight spot, except to say the wrong thing to Melibea and lose what I won by keeping my mouth shut? That's why they say the tambourine is in the hands of her who knows how to play it, and why a practical physician is better than one crammed with book-learning, and why experience makes men wily, and why a wise old woman like me lifts up her skirts when she crosses a stream. Oh my girdle, my girdle! I'll have you bring her to me whether she likes it or not!

SEMPRONIO. Unless I'm going blind, that's Celestina! How the old devil is trotting along talking to herself!

CELESTINA. Why are you crossing yourself, Sempronio? Merely at the sight of me?

SEMPRONIO. I'll tell you. Strange sights cause amazement; amazement conceived in the eyes travels from them to the soul, and the soul manifests it by these external signs. Whoever saw you walking down the street, your head bent, your eyes on the ground, not looking at anyone? Whoever saw you spurring yourself along as if you were on your way to collect a prize? This is odd enough to astonish anyone who knows you. But never mind that and tell me what you've got up your sleeve. Is it a boy or a girl? I've been waiting for you since one o'clock. Your delay is the best sign I can think of.

CELESTINA. That simpleton's rule isn't always to be trusted, my son. If I'd been half an hour later I might have left my nose behind; two hours, my nose and my tongue together! So the longer I took, the more dearly I'd have had to pay.

SEMPRONIO. If you love me, mother, don't leave without telling me!

CELESTINA. Sempronio, my friend, this is not the proper place, and I can't wait anyway. Come with me and we'll tell Calisto something to make him open his eyes. I want him to hear it from my own lips. You'll get some little part of the profit, but I want the thanks for my trouble.

SEMPRONIO. Some *little* part, Celestina? I don't like the sound of that!

CELESTINA. Hush, silly! I'll give you whatever you want. Everything I have is yours. Let's enjoy ourselves together and profit together, and we'll never quarrel. Anyway, we old ones have more needs to meet than you youngsters, especially you who have the table all set for you and don't have to work for your dinner.

SEMPRONIO. I need other things besides food.

CELESTINA. What, my son? Why, ribbons and buckles for your stockings, a band for your hat, and a bow and arrow to go hunting with from house to house, shooting at the little ladybirds in their windows. But alas!, Sempronio, how is an old woman like me going to support herself?

SEMPRONIO. *You false old devil! You bale of corruption! What a greedy-gut you are! She thinks she can take me in as she did my master and get rich at my expense? Well, her money won't do her much good, I can promise her! What a treacherous old wretch! The devil must have got me mixed up with her. I'd have done better to leave this venomous snake alone than to pick her up. It's my fault. Well, I hope she makes enough out of this business, because she's going to keep her word to me, whatever she thinks!*

CELESTINA. What are you saying back there, Sempronio? Were you talking to someone? Why are you hanging back? Hurry!

SEMPRONIO. I was saying, mother, that I'm not surprised at your changeableness, for that's the way women are. Didn't you tell me once that you were going to drag this affair out as long as possible? And now you're running like mad to tell Calisto what happened! You said that the longer we put him off the more he would appreciate it, and that every day we kept him dangling would double our profit.

CELESTINA. The wise man changes his mind; the fool persists. New situations call for new plans. I didn't know, son Sempronio, that I was going to run into such good luck. A good ambassador accommodates himself to circumstances, as I am doing. Moreover, I've heard since that your master is open-handed and capricious. He'll give us more in one day of good tidings than in a hundred while he's suffering and I'm trotting. Unexpected and sudden pleasures are disturbing, and when he's disturbed he can't think. What can come of good but good? What can we expect from a favorable message but a fat reward? So be quiet, fool, and let your old woman operate!

SEMPRONIO. You can at least tell me what you and that noble lady talked about. What did she say? I'm dying to hear it, no less than my master.

CELESTINA. Hush, you idiot! To judge by your red face, you're more anxious to taste this dish than smell it. And now hurry! Your master will be crazy with this delay.

SEMPRONIO. He's crazy without it!

SCENE 2. *Calisto's house. Calisto, Parmeno, Sempronio, Celestina.*

PARMENO. Sir!

CALISTO. What is it, fool?

PARMENO. I see Sempronio and Celestina coming. They're stopping to talk every little while.

CALISTO. You careless oaf! You see them coming and don't run down to open the door? Almighty God! What news are they bringing? They've been gone so long that I was hoping for their return as I hope for salvation. Oh my sad ears, get ready for what's coming! My comfort or my heartache is in Celestina's mouth. If only this short time would pass as swiftly as a dream until I hear her speak! Now I know that it's more painful for a convict to await his sentence than to face the executioner. Parmeno, you sluggard, draw that accursed bolt so this honest old woman can enter at once!

CELESTINA. Do you hear that, Sempronio? Your master's singing a different tune. That's not what we heard him and Parmeno saying the first time we came. Things are improving, I think. Every word he says is worth a new skirt to old Celestina!

SEMPRONIO. When you go in pretend not to see Calisto and say something good.

CELESTINA. Hush, Sempronio! Although I've risked my life, Calisto and his service (and even yours) are worth it, and I expect greater favors from him.

ACT VI

Calisto's house.   Calisto, Celestina,
Parmeno, Sempronio.

CALISTO. What news do you bring, my mother and mistress?

CELESTINA. Oh my lord Calisto, are you here? Oh my fine lover of the beautiful Melibea, and deservedly so! How are you going to reward this old woman who has risked her life for you today? No woman was ever in such a fix! It makes my blood run cold merely to think of it! My life wasn't worth the price of this old frayed cloak!

PARMENO. Lay it on! Give him some bitter along with the sweet! You've moved up a rung; you'll come to the skirt later on. Everything for yourself and nothing for the rest of us! The old woman wants to get in the first bid. She'll prove me right and my master insane. Don't miss anything she says, Sempronio. You'll see she won't ask him for money because it can be divided up.

SEMPRONIO. Shut up, you fool! Calisto will kill you if he hears you!

CALISTO. Dear mother, be brief, I pray you, or take my sword and kill me!

PARMENO. The poor devil's shaking as if he had a chill. He can't stand up. He'd like to lend her his tongue so she could speak more quickly. His life means nothing to him. We'll get a suit of mourning out of this affair, Sempronio!

CELESTINA. Your sword, sir? Save it to use on your enemies. I'm bringing you life and hope from her you love!

CALISTO. Hope?

CELESTINA. You may well call it hope, for she has left the door open against my return! She'd rather see me in this tattered skirt of mine than another in silks and brocades!

PARMENO. Sew up my lips, Sempronio! I can't stand it! She's got round to her skirt already!

SEMPRONIO. Will you keep your mouth shut, or shall I send you to the devil? If she puts in for a skirt, it's because she needs one. She's got to make her living.

PARMENO. And what a living! The old whore wants to make up in one day and in three steps for fifty years of poverty!

SEMPRONIO. Is that what she taught you? Is that the way she raised you?

PARMENO. I can put up with her begging and skinning, but not if it's all for her own pocket.

SEMPRONIO. She's greedy; that's her only weakness. Leave her alone. Let her thatch her own house, and later on she'll thatch ours, or it will be the worse for her.

CALISTO. Tell me, mistress, in God's name, what was she doing? How did you get in? How was she dressed? What part of the house was she in? What was her expression when she greeted you?

CELESTINA. Her expression, sir, was like that of a fierce bull when he faces those who plunge their darts into him in the ring, or like that of a wild boar when he turns on the mastiffs.

CALISTO. And you call that good! What would a bad one be like? It would be death itself! But even death would be a relief to me, better than this torment I'm in!

SEMPRONIO. Is this all that's left of my master's hot fire? What's the matter with him? Hasn't he got the courage to listen to what he wants to hear?

PARMENO. And you told *me* to shut up, Sempronio? If he hears you, you'll catch it no less than I!

SEMPRONIO. Go to hell! He couldn't take offense at what I say, but you haven't got a good word for anybody, you damned, envious troublemaker! I hope you die in some horrible pestilence! Is this what the friendship that Celestina arranged between us amounts to? Get out and bad luck go with you!

CALISTO. My queen and mistress, if you don't want to drive me mad and send my soul to damnation, tell me at once whether your glorious mission was successful or not, and describe the cruel countenance of that avenging angel, which seems to me a sign of hatred rather than love.

CELESTINA. The finest thing about the secret work of the bees (which the discreet should emulate) is that they change everything they touch into something better than it was. Thus have I done with the wild and harsh words of Melibea: I changed her cruelty into honey, her anger into gentleness, her haste into calm. Did you think that old Celestina, whom you rewarded so far beyond her deserts, would do anything else but soften her wrath, put up with her bad temper, be your shield in your absence, and take the blows, the sneers, the insults, the disdain, which all these fillies show at the beginning of love, the more to enhance the value of it? If that were not so, there'd be no difference between the love of prostitutes and that of these sheltered damsels, that is, if they all said "yes" the moment they saw they were being courted. Even though they're on fire with love, modest maidens show a cold face to it, a calm demeanor, a tranquil indifference, a firm spirit and a chaste purpose, and utter words so bitter that their tongues marvel at their hardihood in saying the opposite of what they mean. Be that as it may, in order to give you some measure of repose until I tell you the whole story and the means by which I gained entrance to her house, know that the end of her speech was very good.

CALISTO. Now that you've somewhat reassured me, mistress, you may tell me the worst. Tell me anything you wish and as you wish. I'm all ears. My heart and mind are quieter, my blood is again flowing in my veins, and I'm no longer afraid. We'll go upstairs, if you like, and you can tell me your story there. . . .

Sit down, mistress, and let me kneel and hear her gentle answer. But tell me first how you managed to get in.

CELESTINA. By offering a little thread for sale, a method by which, with the help of God, I've brought down more than thirty of her kind and a few even higher.

CALISTO. They may have been higher in stature, but not in nobility, not in station, grace, or discretion, not in lineage or a becoming haughtiness, not in virtues or sweetness of speech!

PARMENO. The poor fellow's slipping a cog! His clock has stopped at noon and never strikes anything but twelve. Count the strokes, Sempronio. You're fairly drooling, listening to his ravings and her lies!

SEMPRONIO. You poisonous backbiter! Why should you close your ears to what makes the rest of us prick up ours? You're like a snake trying to escape the voice of the charmer. You should be glad to listen to them, however many lies they tell, if only because they're talking about love.

CELESTINA. Listen, my lord Calisto, and you'll hear what your good luck and my diligence have brought to pass. I'd hardly begun to peddle my thread when Melibea's mother was called away to visit a sick sister, and she left Melibea with me.

CALISTO. Oh wonderful! What a heaven-sent opportunity! How I wish I could have been hiding under your cloak!

CELESTINA. Under my cloak, do you say? Alas!, you'd have been seen through thirty holes, unless God sends me a better one.

PARMENO. I'm leaving, Sempronio! I'll not say another word! You listen to it all! If our idiot master weren't so busy measuring in his mind all the steps between here and Melibea's house, and wondering what she looked like, and how she chaffered over the thread, he'd see that my advice would have served him better than Celestina's lies.

CALISTO. What's going on there? Here I am listening to something that means more to me than life itself, and you two whispering as usual, just to annoy me? Be silent, if you love me, and rejoice with me in listening to this good woman, so busy has she been! Tell me, mistress, what did you do when you found yourself alone with her?

CELESTINA. I was so beside myself with joy that anyone could have seen it in my face.

CALISTO. If I am overjoyed merely at hearing it, how much more must you have been in actually seeing such a picture! Weren't you struck dumb by such an unexpected piece of luck?

CELESTINA. On the contrary! I was so anxious to be alone with her that it made me bolder. I opened my heart to her and gave her your message: how you were suffering for lack of a mere word from her to heal you of a grave sickness. And while she was hanging on my words, looking at me, frightened at my strange message, and trying to guess who it was who could be cured in that fashion, I mentioned your name. Whereupon she gave herself a great slap on the forehead, like one who hears a dreadful piece of news, and told me to shut my mouth and get out of her sight, unless I wanted to die by the hands of her servants. And she went on fuming about my effrontery, calling me a witch, a go-between, a false old hag, and many other frightful names such as are used to scare children with.

CALISTO. Tell me all about it, mother. I'm wondering what excuse you could have thought up to quiet her terrible suspicion.

You must be more than woman in your great wisdom! You were ready for her, I'll warrant, for women are nimbler-witted than men in a pinch.

CELESTINA. My excuse, sir? Why, I merely told her that you were suffering from a toothache and that all you wanted from her was a certain prayer she knew.

CALISTO. Marvelous! You haven't your equal in your profession! What a crafty one you are! What quick thinking! I verily believe that if you'd been living in the time of Aeneas and Dido, Venus wouldn't have had to get Dido to love her son Cupid by giving him the form of Ascanius, but could have saved herself the trouble by hiring you as go-between. I'll die happy if I die in such hands as yours! Even if this doesn't turn out as well as I should like, you couldn't have done anything more than you did. What do you think, my lads? Could anyone else have done better? Is there another such woman in the world?

CELESTINA. Don't interrupt me, sir. Let me finish. It's getting late. Evil-doers work at night, and on my way home I might be attacked.

CALISTO. Nonsense! You shall have pages and torches to escort you.

PARMENO. Yes, indeed, so the little girl won't get raped! You go with her, Sempronio. She's afraid of the crickets that sing in the dark.

CALISTO. Did you say something, son Parmeno?

PARMENO. Sir, I said that it will be well for Sempronio and me to go with her, it's so dark.

CALISTO. Good! In a little while. Go on with your story, mother. Tell me what else happened. What did she say when you asked her for the prayer?

CELESTINA. That she would give it to me very gladly.

CALISTO. Gladly? Oh God, what a noble gift!

CELESTINA. I asked her for something else.

CALISTO. What, my honest old friend?

CELESTINA. A silken girdle that she always wears around her waist. I told her it would be good for your toothache because it had touched so many relics.

CALISTO. Go on! What did she say?

CELESTINA. Give me my reward and I'll tell you.

CALISTO. For God's sake, take the whole house and everything in it, and tell me, or ask for anything you like!

CELESTINA. For a cloak that you'll give this old woman she'll give you the very girdle that Melibea wears!

CALISTO. What's this about a cloak? Make it a cloak and a skirt and everything I have!

CELESTINA. I need a cloak and I'll consider myself well paid with it. Don't give me anything else; it would make my request look presumptuous. To offer too much to one who asks for little is a kind of refusal.

CALISTO. Parmeno, run and call my tailor and have him cut a cloak and skirt out of that Flanders cloth he got to make me a cape.

PARMENO. *That's right! Everything for the old woman so she'll come again loaded down with more sweet lies than a honey-bee, and to hell with me! That's what she's been after all day with her dodging around!*

CALISTO. Why the devil are you waiting? Surely, there's no worse served man than I, supporting a lot of star-gazing, grumbling servants who wish me ill! What are you mumbling there, you envious villain? What were you saying? I didn't hear you. Be on your way at once and don't annoy me. I've got enough trouble already. You'll get a coat out of the same piece.

PARMENO. I was only saying, sir, that it's too late to get the tailor.

CALISTO. Didn't I say you're a star-gazer? Well, let it go until tomorrow. And you, my mistress, please bear with me. You'll get your cloak; it's only put off, not lost. And now show me that blessed girdle she wears around her waist. Let my eyes rejoice in the sight of it! My heart hasn't had a moment's rest since I saw that lady, and all my senses have been equally stricken: my eyes in seeing her, my ears in hearing her, and my hands in touching her.

CELESTINA. Touching her, did you say? You astonish me!

CALISTO. In my dreams, I mean.

CELESTINA. Your dreams, sir?

CALISTO. I dream of her so constantly that I fear I'll suffer the fate of Alcibiades or Socrates, the first of whom dreamed that he was wrapped in the cloak of his mistress, and the next day he was killed and there was no one to pick up his body from the street or cover it. Socrates dreamed that someone was calling him, and he died three days later. But dead or alive, I'll be happy if I can wear her girdle!

CELESTINA. You're too easily discouraged. While others rest, you prepare yourself only to endure another day. Courage, sir! God will never abandon His own! See hope in this girdle, for if I live I'll bring its owner to you!

CALISTO. Oh happy girdle, to have encircled the body I'm not worthy to touch! All my hopes are bound up in your knots. Tell me, my girdle, did you hear the distressful answer of your mistress? I serve her night and day and it doesn't avail me.

CELESTINA. An old proverb has it that the less you pursue fortune the sooner you'll overtake her. But I'll do for you what you won't do for yourself. Take comfort, sir, for Zamora was not won in a day.

CALISTO. That doesn't hold for me. Cities are walled with stones and can be taken with stones, but this lady of mine has a heart of steel: no metal can harm it, no cannon dent it. If you set scaling ladders against her walls, her eyes will shoot arrows and her tongue harsh words, and her encampment is so remote that the besiegers can't come within half a league of it.

CELESTINA. Hush, sir. The daring of one man took Troy. Don't despair, for a lone woman can take this city. You've not been at my house; you don't know my arts.

CALISTO. I can believe you, mistress, since you brought me this treasure. Oh glorious girdle that bound that angelic waist! I can't believe my eyes! Oh my girdle, were you my enemy? If you were, say so and I'll forgive you. But you can't have been, for in that event you wouldn't have come to my hands, unless you came to make your excuses. By the great power that your mistress has over me I conjure you, answer me!

CELESTINA. Leave off this raving, sir! I'm worn out with listening to you, as the girdle is with your twisting of it.

CALISTO. Alas, poor wretch that I am! Oh my girdle, would that heaven had made you, not of silk, but of my very flesh, so I might hold each day, with all reverence, those limbs which you unwittingly embrace! Ah, what secrets of that lovely image you must have seen!

CELESTINA. You'll see more, and more sensibly, unless you lose your wits raving!

CALISTO. Hush, mistress. My girdle and I understand each other. Oh my eyes! Remember that it was through you that my heart was pierced. You are to blame for my distemper, but now you can see the physic for it brought to our very door!

SEMPRONIO. Master, you're so in love with the girdle that it almost seems you don't want to enjoy Melibea.

CALISTO. What a mad and babbling killjoy you are! What are you saying?

SEMPRONIO. Why, you talk so much that you'll kill yourself along with everyone in earshot. You'll lose your life or your wits, one or the other. Whichever it is, it's enough to put your light out. Make it short and give Celestina a chance to finish.

CALISTO. Have I annoyed you, mother, with my long speech, or is this lad drunk?

CELESTINA. Even if he is, sir, you should bring your lament to an end. After all, the girdle is only a girdle, not Melibea. Don't treat the person and the garment as equals. You should save something for Melibea when you see her.

CALISTO. Oh my mistress and my comforter, let me console myself with this herald of my glory! Oh my tongue, why do you waste yourself in adoring anything but the excellence of her whom I shall never possess? Oh my hands, how little reverence you have and how carelessly you touch this balm for my wounds! The poisoned arrow can no longer harm me! I am safe, for she who wounded me has sent the cure! Oh my mistress, joy of old women and delight of young ones, repose for the weary, afflict me no further with your fears, but let me feast my eyes upon my treasure and carry it through the streets so that those who see me will know there's no happier man than I!

SEMPRONIO. You only make your sores worse by heaping new desires upon them. Your cure, sir, doesn't depend upon the girdle.

CALISTO. I know it, but I can't help worshipping this token of her.

CELESTINA. Token? That only is a token which is given as a token. Melibea sent you her girdle out of charity, to cure your toothache, not to cure your love-sickness. But if I live I'll make her change her mind!

CALISTO. And the prayer?

CELESTINA. She hasn't given it to me yet.

CALISTO. Why not?

CELESTINA. The time was too short; but she agreed, if you were still suffering, to let me have it tomorrow.

CALISTO. Still suffering? I'll continue to suffer so long as she's cruel to me!

CELESTINA. Enough, sir! We've talked and done enough. She was willing to give me anything I might ask for your toothache. Don't you think I did well for just one visit? I'm leaving now. If you go out tomorrow and happen to pass her door, see that you wear a kerchief around your neck so she'll recognize you and know that my errand was a true one.

CALISTO. I'll wear four of them to please you! But tell me, in God's name, what else did she say? I'm dying to hear words from her sweet mouth. How did you manage to get into her house without knowing her and to come and go so freely?

CELESTINA. Without knowing her, sir? Why, we were neighbors for four years! I used to see them and speak and laugh with them day and night. Her mother knows me better than she knows her own hands, although Melibea has grown up since into a wise and noble woman.

PARMENO. Come closer, Sempronio. I want to whisper something in your ear.

SEMPRONIO. What is it?

PARMENO. Celestina is wasting too much time listening to our master gibbering. Nudge her with your foot and get her on her way. No man is so crazy that he'll talk to himself for long.

CALISTO. Noble, mother? You must be joking! Has she her equal in the whole world? Did God ever create a more beautiful body? Could any painter hope to portray such features, such a model of perfection? Were Helen alive today, she for whom so many Greeks and Trojans died, or the lovely Polixena, daughter of Priam, they would both acknowledge as their better her whom I worship. If she had taken part in the contest of the apple with the three goddesses, it would never have been called the apple of discord, for, without taking offense, they would gladly have awarded it to Melibea and it would have been called the apple of concord. All women who know her curse themselves and complain to God because He forgot them when He made this lady of mine. They're consumed with envy and martyrize their flesh trying to equal with art the perfection that nature gave her. They pluck out their eyebrows with tweezers and gum, and still they fail. They search for herbs, roots, and flowers of golden hue with which to make rinses for their hair so it may resemble hers. They abuse their faces bedaubing them with ointments, salves, and acids, and red and white pastes, which I shall refrain from describing, lest I become tiresome. How could a sad wretch like me hope to serve one who was born with all these gifts?

CELESTINA. I understand, Sempronio. Just leave him alone and he'll fall off his ass. He's almost through.

CALISTO. All nature conspired to make her perfect. Nature distributed her graces among other women, but brought the finest of them together in Melibea, so that those who should see her would know the greatness of her Painter. All she needs is a little pure water and an ivory comb to make her excel all other women in loveliness. These are her weapons; with them she captured me; with them she has tied me as with a strong chain.

CELESTINA. Don't worry yourself further about it. My file is sharp enough to cut your chain and then you'll be free. And now, if you'll permit me, I'll go, for it's very late. And let me take the girdle; I'll need it.

CALISTO. What are you saying? Will my bad luck never cease? With it, or you, or both together, I could have survived this long dark night. But no good thing in this sad life is perfect, so I'll suffer in solitude. Boys!

PARMENO. Sir?

CALISTO. See my mistress home. She takes my joy and pleasure with her, and I remain here alone in sadness.

CELESTINA. God be with you, sir! I'll be back again tomorrow for my cloak and I'll bring her prayer. Be patient, sir, and think of other things.

CALISTO. That I will not do! It would be heresy not to think of the joy of my life!

ACT VII

Scene 1.   *A Street.   Parmeno, Celestina.*

CELESTINA. Parmeno, my son, since last I talked with you I haven't had a chance to prove my love and tell you how well I speak of you even in your absence. I don't have to tell you why, but I considered you as a son, anyway an adopted son, and thought you would be guided by me. But you repaid me by objecting to everything I said, whispering and murmuring against me to Calisto. I didn't think you'd go back on your word, but I see you've still got some foolish notions and like to talk just for the fun of it. This time I want you to listen to me, and remember that I'm an old woman and that good advice dwells in the old, just as pleasure does in the young. I really believe you talked as you did because you're young, but I hope to God, my son, that as you grow up you'll see things differently. Youth is wrapped up in the present, but a riper age sees past, present, and future together. Remember how I loved you, Parmeno, and that my house was your first home in this city. But you youngsters take no account of the old. You live only for your own pleasure and it doesn't occur to you that the flower of your youth will ever wither. But, my friend, you should know that for such needs as these it's good to have one tried friend to go to, a mother and more than a mother, a good inn to stop at when you're well, a good hospital to go to when you're sick, a good purse to draw on when you need money, a good strongbox to keep it in when you've got it, a good fire in winter and a pleasant shade in sum-

mer, and a good tavern to eat and drink in. What do you say to
that, my little madcap? I know by all the talking you did today
that you're all mixed up. I ask of you only what God asks of a
sinner: that he repent and mend his ways. Look at Sempronio.
With God's help I made a man of him. I want you two to be
brothers. If you stand in with him you'll stand in with your
master and everybody else. See how well he's thought of! How
diligent, how courteous, how willing to serve! He needs your
friendship. If you two will join hands you'll both be the gainers
and your master's only counsellors. You must love if you would
be loved. You can't catch trout without getting your breeches
wet. Sempronio owes you nothing, so it's foolishness for you not
to love him in exchange for his love. It's silly to repay friendship
with hatred.

PARMENO. Mother, just between us, I confess I did you wrong
and I hope you'll forgive me. I'll obey you in the future. But I
think it's impossible for me and Sempronio to be friends. He
babbles too much and I'm too impatient with him. How can you
make friends out of two such?

CELESTINA. You once had a different disposition.

PARMENO. Upon my word, the longer I know him the less patience I've got with him. I *am* different. Sempronio hasn't got
anything *I* want.

CELESTINA. A true friend stands by when things get difficult; he
proves himself in adversity. Then it is that he visits more cheerfully the house that fortune has abandoned. Oh what I could tell
you, my son, of the virtues of a good friend! Nothing is rarer or
more to be cherished; he refuses no burden. You two are equals;
you have the same habits; your hearts are alike, and your hearts
are what will keep your friendship alive. Your money, my son, is
in good hands. Earn more if you like, but your fortune is await-
ing you. God bless your good father who made it! But I can't
give it to you until you grow up and lead a more quiet life.

PARMENO. What do you call a quiet life, aunt?

CELESTINA. Making your own living, my son, not in other people's houses, which you'll always be doing unless you learn how to get properly paid for your services. Why, seeing you in rags today, I felt so sorry for you that I begged Calisto to give you a coat, not just to give me a cloak. I mean that when the tailor comes, your master, seeing you've got no coat, will give you one. So I didn't act solely for my own profit, as I heard you say, but for yours also. If you wait for the usual thanks of these gallants, you could put in a handbag everything you'd get in ten years. Enjoy your youth while you may, your good days and better nights, your good eating and drinking. Don't give it up, whatever the price. Don't be envious of your master's wealth, for envy will take you from this world which you've got only one lifetime to enjoy. Oh Parmeno, my son, and I can well call you my son, having raised you for such a long while, take my advice which I give you because I want you to cut a figure in the world. How happy I'd be if you and Sempronio were very close, very good friends! Brothers in everything, coming to my poor house to enjoy yourselves and even to frolic a bit with my girls.

PARMENO. Your girls, mother?

CELESTINA. To be sure! I said girls, for old women like me aren't good for that kind of thing. I gave Sempronio one of them, and I don't love him as much as I love you. I speak straight from my heart, Parmeno.

PARMENO. You may be making a mistake, mistress.

CELESTINA. Even if I were I'd not regret it, for I'd also be acting for the love of God, seeing you alone in a strange land, and especially for your father's sake who gave you in my charge. One of these days you'll be a man with a riper understanding and you'll say: "Old Celestina was right!"

PARMENO. Even though I'm not grown up yet, I'm sorry I said what I did today. I said it, not so much because I didn't like what you were doing, but because I gave my master some good advice and he thanked me so badly for it. But from now on we'll hunt together. You do your work and I'll keep my mouth shut. I was caught once by ignoring your advice in this business.

CELESTINA. You'll be caught again if you don't listen to me. I'm a true friend to you.

PARMENO. I'm beginning to see that the time I spent in your service was well spent, it's paying off so handsomely. I'll pray God for the peace of my father's soul for giving me such a guardian, and for that of my mother's also, for leaving me in the hands of such a woman!

CELESTINA. In God's name, my son, don't speak of her! You bring tears to my eyes. When did I ever have another such friend, another such companion, another such comforter in trouble, as my sister and your mother, who covered my faults and shared my secrets, and who was all my joy and repose? How brave she was, how sincere, how virile! She'd go out as fearlessly by night from cemetery to cemetery looking for the materials of our trade as if it were day. She didn't spare the graves of Christian, Jew, or Moor, but saw them buried by day and dug them up by night! She loved the dark as you love the light and always said it was the sanctuary of sinners. And how clever she was along with her other talents! Let me tell you something to show you what a mother you lost, although it shouldn't be told, but then I can be free with you. Well, she extracted seven teeth from a hanged man with a pair of tweezers while I was removing his shoes! She was better at calling up the devil than I was, although I was better known for it then than I am now, because her art perished with her, for my sins. In short, the very devils themselves were afraid of her, she scared them so with her blood-curdling screams. In fact, she was as familiar with them as you are with the members of your own household, and when she called them up they'd come tumbling over each other. They didn't dare lie to her, such was her power over them. After I lost her I never knew one of them to tell the truth.

PARMENO. *Damn this old hag! She's certainly out to please me with her praises of my mother!*

CELESTINA. What are you saying, my honest Parmeno, my more than son?

PARMENO. I was saying, how could my mother have been better at it than you, since you both used the same spells?

CELESTINA. Does that surprise you? You know the old saying, that there's a great difference between Peter and Peter. Not many of us ever attained my gossip's eminence. Haven't you noticed that in all trades some are better than others? That's how it was with your mother (may she rest in peace!), for she was the first in our profession and was known and loved by everyone: gentlemen and priests, married men, old men, youths, and children. And housemaids and virgins? Why, they prayed for her as they prayed for their own parents! She was useful to all of them and they treated her like one of the family. When we went down the street everyone we met was a godchild of hers, for her principal occupation for sixteen years was midwifery. You knew none of this then, for you were too small, but it's now time for you to know her secrets, for she is dead and you are a man grown.

PARMENO. Tell me, mistress, when you were arrested that time, when I was living with you, were you and my mother well up in your art?

CELESTINA. Are you joking? We practiced it together, we were overheard together, arrested together, accused together, and together we were sentenced. That was the first time, I think. But you were very young and I'm surprised you remember it, for nothing is more forgotten in this whole city. Those are just things that happen in this world. Every day you'll see people do wrong and pay for it, if you care to look around for such things.

PARMENO. That's true, but they say that in sin the worst thing is to persevere in it. Just as a man's first movement is not in his control, neither is his first mistake. That's why they say that he who sins and repents, commends himself to God.

CELESTINA. *You reached me that time, little fool! So you want the truth, do you? Wait a bit and I'll give you more than you bargained for!*

PARMENO. What did you say, mother?

CELESTINA. I was saying, my son, that, not counting that occasion, they arrested your mother (whom God cherish!) four other times. Once they accused her of being a witch, because they found her working by candle-light at a crossroads one night digging up earth, and she had to spend half a day perched on a ladder in the public square, with a painted witch's cap on her head. But these are trifles. We have to put up with such things in this world to make a living. And how little did she mind it, with her good sense! She didn't give up her profession on that account, not she! She even got better at it. So much for what you said about persevering in sin. She was good at everything. Before God and my conscience, so calm was she, even on her ladder, that you'd have thought she despised the people down below! And so it is that those who, like her, are worthy and wise and amount to something, are the very ones who soonest go wrong. Look at Virgil, how wise he was! And yet you must have heard how he was left hanging in a basket with all Rome gazing at him. But he was not the less honored on that account, nor did he lose the name of Virgil.

PARMENO. What you say is true, but he wasn't hung up there by the authorities.

CELESTINA. Hush, fool! What do you know about it? Is it better to suffer for transgressing the law than for some other reason? That priest (may he rest in peace!) knew better who, when they came to console him at his execution, said that the Scriptures hold those blessed who suffer persecution by the authorities, for theirs will be the kingdom of heaven. Consider whether it's such a grave matter to suffer a bit in this world in order to win glory in the next, especially in your mother's case, for she was wrongfully and unreasonably accused, with false witnesses, and with cruel tortures was forced to confess to being what she was not.

But she had courage and a heart inured to suffering, which makes things seem lighter than they are, and so she gave not a fig for it all. Why, I've heard her say a thousand times: "What if they did break my foot on the rack, it was all to the good, for now I'm more famous than I was!" Well then, since your mother had such a rough time on earth, we must believe that God made it up to her in heaven, if what that priest said is true, and that is of some comfort to me. Strive to be good, like her, a true friend to me, for you've got someone to take after. What your father left you is in safe hands.

PARMENO. I believe you, mother, but I'd like to know how much it is.

CELESTINA. Not now; all in good time, as I told you.

PARMENO. Never mind the dead and their money. If I was left nothing I shall inherit nothing. Let's talk about immediate matters, which are of more concern to us than recollections of the past. You remember, don't you, that not long ago you promised me I should have Areusa, that time at my house when I told you I was crazy about her?

CELESTINA. Yes, I promised; I haven't forgotten it. Don't think I've lost my memory with age. I've jogged myself about it three times since then and I think she must be ripe by now. Let's get along to her house. She can hardly hold out any longer. That's the least I'll do for you.

PARMENO. I was getting discouraged. I couldn't even get her to speak to me. It's a bad sign, as the saying goes, when they shy at love, so I was feeling pretty sick about it.

CELESTINA. Don't take it so hard. You don't know me or how well you stand with the head of this shop. But now you'll see what I can do for you, how much I know about love, and how much water I draw with my girls. Here's her door. Go in quietly so her friends won't hear you. Wait under the staircase while I go up and see what can be done in our little affair. Perhaps more than we thought!

SCENE 2. *Areusa's house. Areusa,*
Celestina, Parmeno.

AREUSA. Who is it? Who's coming up to my room at this time of night?

CELESTINA. One who doesn't hate you, certainly, one who never takes a step without thinking of your good, one who remembers you better than herself, your sweetheart, even though an old woman.

AREUSA. *The devil take the old crone! Stalking around like a ghost at this hour!* Aunt, mistress, you're very welcome, even if it is late. I was undressing to go to bed.

CELESTINA. With the chickens, daughter? What a way to make your fortune! Get up and bestir yourself! Let others complain of being poor, but not you! I bring home the hay and you eat it. Anyone would prefer that kind of life!

AREUSA. Jesus! Let me put my clothes on! I'm freezing!

CELESTINA. Do nothing of the kind, my dear. Just get into bed and you can talk from there.

AREUSA. I will, for I've been ailing all day. I was so cold that I had to wrap myself in the sheets.

CELESTINA. Well, don't sit up in bed. Get under the covers. You look like a siren.

AREUSA. Whatever you say, aunt.

CELESTINA. How sweet your bed smells when you move! It's lovely! I always did like the way you do things, your neatness and style. You're a sweet thing. God bless you! What sheets and what a quilt! How white they are! May my old age be as nice! You can see how much I love you if I came to see you at this hour.

Let me look you over and take my time about it, I'm so pleased with you.

AREUSA. Gently, mother! Don't touch me. You'll tickle me and make me laugh, and when I laugh I hurt worse.

CELESTINA. Where do you hurt, my love? You aren't joking, are you?

AREUSA. May I drop dead if I'm joking! For the last four hours I've been sick with the vapors, and they've got up to my breasts and I hurt so badly I think I'm dying. But I'm not as old as you think!

CELESTINA. Move over and let me explore a bit. For my sins I know something about that trouble; we all have to go through it.

AREUSA. It's higher up, over the stomach.

CELESTINA. God and St. Michael bless you, my angel! And how plump and fresh you are! What breasts! Beautiful! I thought you were good-looking before, seeing only the surface, but now I can tell you that in this whole city, so far as I know, there aren't three such figures as yours! You don't look a day over fifteen! I wish I were a man and could look at you! By God, you're committing a sin not to share your beauty with those who love you! God didn't give you such youthful freshness to hide under six layers of wool and linen. Don't be stingy with what has cost you so little. Why hoard your beauty, which circulates as readily as money? Don't be a dog in the manger. You can't enjoy your own good looks, so let those enjoy them who can. Do you think you were created without a purpose? When a girl is born a boy is born, one for the other. Everything in this world was made with some design and nature has a use for it. It's a sin to vex men when you can help them.

AREUSA. You praise me, mother, but no man loves me. Don't mock me, but give me some medicine for my sickness.

CELESTINA. We women are all experts in that disease, sinner that I am! I'll tell you what I've seen others do and what has always helped me, although it may not help you, for people have different constitutions and medicines affect them differently. All strong smells are good, such as makebate, wormwood, smoke of partridge feathers, rosemary, musk, and incense. If you sniff them frequently they'll put the uterus back in place and stop your pain. But there's another remedy, however, which I've always found better than anything else, but I won't tell you what it is, you've turned so holy on me.

AREUSA. What is it, mother, if you love me? Here I am suffering and you won't help me?

CELESTINA. Come, come! You understand me well enough. Don't play the fool!

AREUSA. Oh that! Damn me if I knew what you were driving at! But what do you expect me to do? My lover left yesterday for the wars with his captain. Do you want me to play him false?

CELESTINA. Bah! Play him false! What harm would you be doing?

AREUSA. Plenty, because he gives me everything I need. He keeps me in style and treats me as if I were his wife.

CELESTINA. Even so, unless you have a baby you'll always be sick as you are now, and he's probably to blame for it.

AREUSA. It's only my bad luck, a curse my parents put on me. Didn't you know all that? But let's drop it; it's late. Tell me what you came up for.

CELESTINA. You remember what I told you about Parmeno? Well, he's complaining that you won't see him—I don't know why, unless it's out of spite for me because you know I love him and consider him my son. I've got my own ideas about your whims. Your sisters do better. It does me good to see them. I know they've talked to you.

AREUSA. I don't think you're right about me, aunt.

CELESTINA. I don't know. I believe in deeds; you can buy words cheaply anywhere. You can repay love only with love, and deeds with deeds. Well, you and Elicia are cousins, you know, and she has accepted Sempronio. He and Parmeno are cronies; they work for that gentleman I've told you about. You could have a lot of influence with him. You can't refuse to do what will cost you nothing. You and Elicia, cousins; the other two, chums. Don't you see how beautifully it all fits? . . . Parmeno came with me. Shall I call him up?

AREUSA. Oh my goodness! Suppose he's been listening!

CELESTINA. No; he's downstairs. I want you to have him up. Welcome him; greet him cheerfully and show him a smiling face. And if you like his looks, enjoy him and let him enjoy you. Even though he gets something out of it, you won't lose anything.

AREUSA. I know well enough, mistress, that your advice has always been for my own good, but how can you expect me to do such a thing when I've got to answer for it to my other man? If he hears of it he'll kill me. And my sisters will tell him, they're so envious of me. Even if I only lose him, it will be more than I stand to gain by taking on Parmeno.

CELESTINA. Don't worry about that. We came in very quietly.

AREUSA. I don't mean just for tonight, but for many other nights.

CELESTINA. What! Are you one of those? Is that the way you look after yourself? You'll never have a decent place of your own. If you're afraid of him when he's away, what will you do when he's in town? It's my bad luck always to be wasting advice on fools! They go wrong in spite of it. But I'm not surprised: the world is big and the number of the wise is small. Ah, my daughter, if you only knew how sharp your cousin is and how well she has done for herself by taking my advice, and how high she has climbed in her profession! She hasn't done badly at all! She keeps one in her bed, one at the door, and a third sighing for her, all at the same time. And she does right by all of them and smiles upon them, and they all think she loves them, and each believes he's the only one and her favorite, and gives her whatever she wants. If you had two lovers do you imagine that the slats of your bed would give you away? How can you support yourself by a single small dribble? You'll never have anything to spare. I'll not want your leftovers! I never cared for one man alone. Two can do more for you, and four still more. They've got more to give and you've got more to choose among. The most miserable creature in the world is the mouse who knows only one hole, for if it's sealed up he's got no place to hide in from the cat. The one-eyed man, how dangerously does he travel! A soul alone neither sings nor weeps. A single action doesn't make a habit. You'll rarely see a partridge flying by itself, especially in summer. You'll hardly ever see a friar alone in the street. What's so fine about this number one? I could tell you more things wrong with it than I've got years to my back. It's much better to have at least two for the sake of good company, two such as Parmeno. . . . Come up, my son.

AREUSA. No, no! Damn my soul, I'll die of shame! I've never met him; I was always too shy.

CELESTINA. Well, I'll cure you. I'll talk for the two of you. After all, he's as scared as you are.

PARMENO. Mistress, may God bless your gracious presence!

AREUSA. You're welcome, sir!

CELESTINA. Come closer, you ass! Were you going to sit in the corner? What are you scared of? Remember what they say, that the devil brought the bashful man to the palace for his undoing. Now, you two listen to me. Parmeno, my friend, you know what I promised you; and you, my daughter, know what I asked you to do. Never mind now about your objections; we haven't got time to waste in palaver. Parmeno has always been crazy about you, and you, seeing him in pain, won't want him to die, I know. I can see already that you like him well enough to let him stay here tonight.

AREUSA. Oh no, Mother! Please! Jesus! Don't make me do that!

PARMENO. Mother, for the love of God get her to agree to something before I go! Just seeing her has set me on fire. Offer her everything my father left me! Tell her she can have whatever I've got! Go on now, tell her! She won't even look at me!

AREUSA. What's that gentleman whispering to you? Does he think I've got to do everything you say?

CELESTINA. He was saying, daughter, that he's happy in your friendship because you're such an honest girl, and how glad he'd be to give you anything you like. He also said that he'll be a good friend to Sempronio because he wants to please me, and that he'll agree to whatever Sempronio may do in a certain business we've got on hand with his master. Isn't that so, Parmeno? Have I got your word for it?

PARMENO. Of course!

CELESTINA. *Ha, sir rascal, I've got you now! I caught you at the proper moment!* Come here, you awkward clodhopper! I want to see what you can do before I go. Roll her on the bed!

AREUSA. He wouldn't be so impolite! I haven't given him permission!

CELESTINA. What's this about politeness and permissions? Well, I won't wait around any longer, for I know you'll get up in the morning a bit pale but cured of your trouble. But this fellow! He's a little bugger, a fighting cock, and you won't make him lower his crest in three nights on end! In my day, down in my country, the doctors used to send me his kind to eat. But I had better teeth in those days! Good-bye now! I can't stand your kissing and frolicking. I've still got the taste of it in my mouth, although I lost my teeth long ago!

AREUSA. God go with you!

PARMENO. Mother, don't you want me to see you home?

CELESTINA. You'd only be swapping the devil for a witch. God will see me home. I don't think they'll rape me in the street, I'm that old!

SCENE 3. *Celestina's house.*
Celestina, Elicia.

ELICIA. What's the dog barking about? I'll bet it's that old devil!

CELESTINA. (Knocks.)

ELICIA. Who is it? Who's knocking?

CELESTINA. Come down and let me in, daughter.

ELICIA. How you run around! How you love to gad at night! Why do you do it? Why were you gone so long, mother? You never go out just to come back again. It's a habit. You keep your word with one customer and leave a hundred complaining. Today the father of that girl who's getting married was looking for you—the girl, you remember, you took to the almoner last Sunday. Her father wants to get her married off three days from now; but she's got to be patched up first, as you promised, so her husband won't notice anything missing.

CELESTINA. I don't remember anyone like that, daughter.

ELICIA. You don't remember? You're certainly getting absent-minded! Your memory's going back on you. Why, you told me when you took her to the almoner you'd patched her up seven times already!

CELESTINA. Don't be surprised, daughter. I've got so many things on my mind that some of them get away from me. Are they coming back?

ELICIA. What a question! They give you a gold bracelet on account and you wonder if they're coming back!

CELESTINA. Oh, the girl with the gold bracelet? I remember now. But why didn't you start to work on her? You need to practice what you've seen me do so many times. If you don't, you'll be a donkey for the rest of your life, without a proper trade or any money coming in. And when you get to be as old as I am you'll be sorry you were so lazy. Idleness in youth brings repentance in old age. I did better when your grandmother (may God cherish her!) was teaching me my trade. After a year I was better at it than she was.

ELICIA. I'm not surprised, for they say the pupil often betters his instruction. But that only happens when the pupil is willing to learn. Teaching is wasted on the unwilling. I hate this trade of yours and you're crazy about it—there's the difference!

CELESTINA. So much the worse for you. Do you want to spend your old age in poverty? Do you think I'll always be here to look after you?

ELICIA. For God's sake let's drop the arguments and the sermons and enjoy ourselves while we may! Eat today and let tomorrow take care of itself! The man who makes a lot of money dies as quickly as the poor man, the doctor as quickly as the shepherd, the pope as the sexton, the lord as the serf, the man of high station as the villain, you with your trade as I without it. We can't live forever. Let's be merry, for few of us will reach old age and none of those who do will have died of hunger. And now to bed; it's time!

ACT VIII

SCENE 1.   *Areusa's house.   Parmeno,*
Areusa.

PARMENO. It can't be morning already! What's that bright light?

AREUSA. What do you mean, morning? Go back to sleep, sir; we just now went to bed. I've hardly closed my eyes. How could it be morning? Open the window there, for God's sake, and you'll see that it's still dark outside.

PARMENO. I was right, mistress; it's broad day! What a miserable servant I am! How badly I've treated my master! I ought to be whipped! How late it is!

AREUSA. Late?

PARMENO. Very late.

AREUSA. The devil take me! I'm still sick! I can't understand it!

PARMENO. What do you want to do, my life?

AREUSA. Talk about my trouble.

PARMENO. My dear lady, if we haven't talked about it enough already you'll have to excuse me, for it's noon. If I get home any later my master won't like it a bit. I'll come again tomorrow and whenever you want me. Maybe that's why God made the days follow each other, so that what isn't done in one can be finished in the next. Here's a little present for you so we'll meet again. Will you eat with us today at Celestina's house?

AREUSA. Yes, and thank you very much! Go now with God and close the door behind you!

PARMENO. God be with you!

SCENE 2.   *A street.   Parmeno.*

PARMENO. Oh wonderful night! No luckier man was ever born! To think I got such a present free, just for the asking! If I could put up with that old woman's hocus-pocus I'd go to her on my knees! How can I repay her? Who can I talk to about it? Oh Lord, who can I get to share my secret? She was right: no pleasure is complete without company. If you keep it to yourself it's not pleasure. But who could relish my good fortune as much as I do? Ah, there's Sempronio at the door. He's up early! If my master has gone out I'm in for it! But he hasn't; it's not his habit. On the other hand, since he's out of his wits these days, I shouldn't be surprised if he has gone.

SCENE 3.   *Calisto's house.   Sempronio, Parmeno, Calisto.*

SEMPRONIO. Brother Parmeno, if I knew where that land is where you can earn your living sleeping I'd give a good deal to go there! I wouldn't give up my place to anyone and I'd earn as much as the best! You lazy lout, why did you go away and not come back? The only way I can account for it is that you must have stayed with the old woman last night to keep her warm and tickle her feet, as you used to do when you were a youngster.

PARMENO. Oh Sempronio, my friend and more than brother, don't spoil things, please! Don't ruin everything with your bad temper. Don't scold me. Be kind to me and I'll tell you about my wonderful adventure last night.

SEMPRONIO. Let's have it. Did you sleep with Melibea?

PARMENO. Melibea! I should say not! It was someone I love better, someone who, if I'm not mistaken, is just as beautiful. Not all the good looks in the world are locked up in Melibea, I can tell you!

SEMPRONIO. What are you raving about, idiot? I'd like to laugh, but I can't. So we're all lovers now! The world is certainly going to the dogs! Calisto and Melibea, me and Elicia, and now you come along just to be in the swim and lose what little sense you've got over some girl!

PARMENO. Is it so silly of me to fall in love?

SEMPRONIO. It is, if you believe your own words. I heard you giving Calisto a lot of foolish advice, contradicting Celestina in everything she said, and then, just to keep her and me from getting anything out of it, you refused to go in with us. Well, now I've got you where I want you and I'm going to make you sweat!

PARMENO. It isn't a proof of great strength or power, Sempronio, to hurt and do harm to others, but rather to do good and help them, and, even better, to have the will to do so. I've always thought of you as my brother. For God's sake don't prove the proverb right that says: great friends fall out over small matters. You're treating me very badly and I don't know why.

SEMPRONIO. I've got reason to. You'd better put another sardine in the pot for the stable boy if you're going to stay out all night with your mistress.

PARMENO. Go on and scold me. I'll take even worse from you.

SEMPRONIO. You treated Calisto worse, telling him not to love Melibea, playing the saint, acting like the signboard of an inn, which can't shelter itself but gives shelter to everyone else.

. . . Ah, Parmeno, now you can see how easy it is to correct others and how hard it is to correct ourselves! Don't say any more! You're the living proof of it! Well, we'll see how you act from now on, for you've got your finger in the pie along with the rest of us. If you had been my friend when I needed you, you'd have backed Celestina and not put in those nasty comments about everything she did. When the wine gets down to the dregs the drinkers leave the tavern. In the same way false friends desert you when you're in trouble and show their true colors.

PARMENO. I once heard, and now I know it from experience, that we never have any pleasure without its corresponding worry. Dark clouds and rain follow the clear and happy sunshine; pain and death, our solace and delight; tears and pain, our joy and laughter; anxiety and gloom, our rest and peace. Who could have been happier than I was just now, and who could have had a worse home-coming? Who could have had a more wonderful night than I had with my dear Areusa, and how quickly you spoiled it! You haven't given me a chance to tell you I'm now on your side and that I'll support you in everything you do, and how sorry I am for what I did, and how much good advice Celestina gave me; that is, she told me this affair of our master and Melibea is in our hands now and we'd better make a killing while the going is good.

SEMPRONIO. I like your words well enough if you'll back them up. I'll believe you when you do. But what were you saying about Areusa? Do you mean Elicia's cousin?

PARMENO. Well, what do you think I was so happy about? I had her!

SEMPRONIO. How the fool talks! He can hardly speak from laughing. What do you mean, you had her? Did you see her at her window, or what?

PARMENO. I mean I left her wondering whether she was going to have a baby or not!

SEMPRONIO. Well, well! It only goes to show what you can do if you keep at a thing! The dropping of water, etc.

PARMENO. You'll see how long I had to keep at it. I only heard of her yesterday for the first time and last night I slept with her!

SEMPRONIO. I see the old woman's hand in this.

PARMENO. How?

SEMPRONIO. Oh, she told me how much she loved you and what she was going to do for you. You're the lucky one! You no sooner arrive than you move in! That's why they say it's better to have God on your side than to get up early. You had a good backer!

PARMENO. Yes, if you pick out a good tree you'll enjoy the shade. I came late but got in early. Oh brother! What I could tell you of Areusa's talents and the rest! But we'd better leave it for some other time.

SEMPRONIO. Well, after all, she's Elicia's cousin. You can't tell me she's got anything that Elicia hasn't. I believe you. But how much did it cost you? Did you pay her anything?

PARMENO. Not a penny! But it would have been worth it if I had! She's got everything! She could get any price she asked! She's an exception to the rule that you never get something for nothing. I invited her to eat at Celestina's today, and, if you like, we'll all go together.

SEMPRONIO. Who, brother?

PARMENO. Why, you and me and Areusa. The old woman and Elicia will be there anyway. We'll have a good time.

SEMPRONIO. That's wonderful! And generous of you! I'll never let you down. You've grown up. Forget my irritation. You're going in with us and everything will turn out all right. I love you! Let me embrace you! Let's be brothers and let the devil go chase himself! Our little disagreement was nothing but a summer's quarrel, peace for the rest of the year. As they say, the squabbles of friends are the renewal of love. Let's eat and be merry, and let our master do the fasting for us!

PARMENO. What's the poor fool doing?

SEMPRONIO. He's stretched out on the sofa, just where you left him last night. He hasn't slept, nor has he been awake. When I go in he begins to snore; when I go out he sings or raves. I can't find out whether he's suffering from love, or resting from it.

PARMENO. Hasn't he called me or missed me?

SEMPRONIO. Why, he doesn't even remember himself, so how could he remember you?

PARMENO. This is my lucky day! But just in case he happens to think of me, I'll send in his breakfast. They'd better get it ready.

SEMPRONIO. What are you planning to give those two little hare-brains of ours for dinner, to show them you know how to do things properly?

PARMENO. When the house is full the dinner is soon prepared. There's enough in the pantry to keep us from disappointing them: white bread, wine from Monviedro, and a leg of pork, besides the six brace of fowl that our master's tenants brought him the other day. And those pigeons he ordered for today, I'll tell him they were beginning to stink. You'll back me up. We'll fix it so he won't get sick from over-eating and we'll have a proper dinner ourselves. Later we'll talk over our business with the old woman and see what we can get out of this affair of our master's.

SEMPRONIO. Out of his trouble, you mean. This time he's going to end up either mad or dead! Well, that's settled. Hurry now! Let's see what he's up to.

CALISTO.

> *My agony will soon be over;*
> *My death I soon expect to see;*
> *My desire is still demanding*
> *What my hope denies to me!*

PARMENO. Listen, Sempronio! Our master is versifying!

SEMPRONIO. What a minstrel! What a son of a whore! A second Antipater of Sidon, a second Ovid, who spoke in verse! Yes, indeed! The devil will be riming next! He's raving in his sleep.

CALISTO.

> *How well thou dost to grieve*
> *And live in pain, my heart!*
> *Too soon didst thou fall victim*
> *To Cupid's golden dart!*

PARMENO. Didn't I tell you?

CALISTO. Who's that talking? Boys!

PARMENO. Sir?

CALISTO. Is it late? Is it time to go to bed?

PARMENO. It's a bit late to be getting up!

CALISTO. What are you saying, fool? Don't tell me the night is gone!

PARMENO. And a good part of the day as well!

CALISTO. Sempronio, is this idiot telling me the truth, trying to make me believe it's day?

SEMPRONIO. Put Melibea out of your mind for a moment, sir, and you'll see the light. You've been staring at her face so much that you're dazzled, like a partridge by the lantern of the hunter.

CALISTO. I believe you now; I hear the church bells. Give me my clothes. I'll go to Mass at the Magdalene and pray God to guide Celestina's steps and soften Melibea's heart, or to put an end to my life.

SEMPRONIO. Don't vex yourself so much. Don't try to get everything at once. It isn't wise to be in such a hurry to get something which may turn out badly anyway. If you insist on having a thing done in a day which could easily take a year, you won't live long.

CALISTO. You mean I'm as impatient as the Galician squire's boy who went barefoot all the year and then, one day, just because his shoes weren't ready, tried to kill the cobbler?

SEMPRONIO. God forbid! You are my master! Besides, I know you'd punish me for my impudence, just as you'd reward me for my good advice, although it's true that one's reward for good service or right speaking is never so great as one's punishment for wrong doing or wrong speaking.

CALISTO. Who taught you all your philosophy, Sempronio?

SEMPRONIO. Sir, what is not black is not necessarily white. My words only seem wise because your reason is befuddled by impatience. When you first saw Melibea you should have had her brought to you all wrapped up and tied with her girdle, just like any other piece of merchandise you might buy in the marketplace, and then the only trouble you'd have would be to pay the bill. Don't be so gloomy, sir. You can't squeeze a great stroke of good fortune into a small space. An oak is not felled by a single blow of the axe. Patience is the proper armor to wear for a rough battle like this.

CALISTO. You'd be right if my patience were strong enough.

SEMPRONIO. What are your wits for, sir, if you let your desires drive you mad?

CALISTO. Oh you fool! The healthy man says to the sick one: God give you health! I don't want any more of your advice or arguments, which only make me worse. I'm going to Mass alone and I'll not be back until you come and claim your reward for telling me of Celestina's success. I'll not eat till then, even though Apollo's horses have been put out to pasture after their daily run.

SEMPRONIO. Leave off these high-flown phrases, sir, this poetizing. Speech that's not common to all, or shared by all, or understood by all, is not good speech. Just say "until sunset" and we'll know what you mean. And eat a bit of conserve to keep you going all that while.

CALISTO. Sempronio, my faithful servant, my good counsellor, my loyal friend, I'll do as you think best. I know from your blameless service that you love my life as you love your own.

SEMPRONIO. Do you agree with him, Parmeno? I'll bet you wouldn't swear to it! And when you go for the conserve don't forget to lift a jar of it for our little ones, who mean a bit more to us than he does. A word to the wise. . . . You can hide it in your breeches.

CALISTO. What are you saying, Sempronio?

SEMPRONIO. I was telling Parmeno to get you a slice of conserve.

PARMENO. Here it is, sir.

CALISTO. Give it to me.

SEMPRONIO. Look how the poor devil is gobbling it! He wants to swallow it whole so he can be on his way.

CALISTO. That saved my life! Good-bye, my lads! Wait for the old one and come for your reward.

PARMENO. The devil go with him, and bad luck too! He ate the conserve as eagerly as Apuleius ate the poison that changed him into an ass!

ACT IX

Scene 1. *A street. Sempronio, Parmeno.*

SEMPRONIO. Fetch our capes and swords, Parmeno, if you please. It's time to go.

PARMENO. Let's hurry. They'll be complaining because we're late. . . . Not down that street; let's take this other one that goes past the church. If Celestina has finished her devotions we'll take her along.

SEMPRONIO. A fine time for her to be praying!

PARMENO. What is good to do at any time can't be untimely.

SEMPRONIO. You're right, of course, but you don't know Celestina as I know her. When she's got a job to do she doesn't worry about priests or piety. If there's a bone to gnaw on at home the saints are safe, but when she goes to church, beads in hand, it means the cupboard is bare. She raised you, but I know her better. She uses her beads to count the number of maidenheads she's got on hand for repair, how many lovers there are in the city, how many girls she has contracted for, and what almoners and canons are the youngest and most free with their money. When she moves her lips she's rehearsing lies and thinking up new schemes to make a penny: "I'll attack him from this angle; he'll say this or that; I'll reply thus." That's how our honest friend makes her living.

PARMENO. I could add something to that, but I won't, because you got so angry with me yesterday when I told Calisto about her.

SEMPRONIO. Knowing something useful doesn't mean you've got to publish it to your own hurt. If our master knew what we know about her he'd throw her out; and if he got rid of her he'd have to hire another to take her place, and we couldn't expect to get our share out of it as we do with Celestina, who in one way or another is going to give us our part of her earnings.

PARMENO. I agree. But hush now! Her door is open. She's at home. You'd better knock before you go in, just in case they're busy and don't want to be interrupted.

SEMPRONIO. Come on! Don't worry; we're all in the family. They're setting the table.

SCENE 2.   *Celestina's house.   Sempronio,
Parmeno, Celestina, Elicia,
Areusa, Lucrecia.*

CELESTINA. Oh my gilded pearls! You're as welcome as I hope this coming year will be!

PARMENO. What a noble speech! Listen to her false flattery, brother!

SEMPRONIO. Leave her alone. That's her trade. But I wonder who the devil taught her so much crookedness!

PARMENO. Necessity, poverty, and hunger. There are no better teachers in the world, nothing that wakes up and sharpens the wits so well. What else taught the magpies and parrots to imitate our speech with their silvery tongues?

CELESTINA. Girls! Girls! You idiots! Come at once! Two men are down here trying to rape me!

ELICIA. I wish they'd stayed at home! What's the good of inviting people to dinner ahead of time? My cousin's been here for three hours! It's the fault of that lazy Sempronio, who can't bear the sight of me lately.

SEMPRONIO. Hush, my mistress, my love, my life! He who serves another is not his own master. My service is my excuse. Don't be angry with me, but let's sit down and eat.

ELICIA. Of course! How prompt he is when it comes to eating! The table's set, his hands are washed, and shame is not in him!

SEMPRONIO. We'll quarrel later, but let's eat now. You sit down first, mother Celestina.

CELESTINA. After you, my sons. There's room for all of us, thank God! I hope we'll have as much in heaven when we get there. Sit down by your girls, and I'll sit here alone with the jug and glass. I can't do anything but talk anyway, and wine is a help. Ever since I got old my best job at the table is pouring the wine, for if you handle honey a little of it is bound to stick to your fingers. There's no better warming pan on a winter's night. If I drink three little jugs like this when I go to bed I don't feel the cold all night long. I line my garments with it at Christmas time. It warms my blood, keeps me from falling to pieces, makes me walk cheerfully, and keeps me young. So long as my house is well supplied with it I'll never fear a lean year. With wine and a mouse-eaten crust I can keep going for three days together.

SEMPRONIO. Aunt, we all like the taste of it, but if we do nothing but eat and drink we won't have time to talk over that affair of our mad master and the gracious and gentle Melibea.

ELICIA. Get away from me, you unmannerly clod! I hope you get a bellyache from your dinner! You've certainly spoiled mine! By my soul, I feel like throwing up what I've eaten, you make me so sick with her gentleness! She's gentle, she is! Jesus! Have you no shame? Who do you call gentle? May I be damned if there's anything gentle about her! Only a person with sore eyes could enjoy looking at such! Your ignorance and stupidity are enough to make me cross myself. I could tell you a thing or two about her beauty and gentleness, but I don't feel up to it! So Melibea's gentle, is she? Yes, she'll be gentle when the Ten Commandments get up and walk two by two! You can buy her kind of beauty for a penny in any shop. I know plenty of girls living on her own street that God made better-looking than Melibea! The only reason you think she's beautiful is because she's all decked out in fine clothes. Hang them on a clothes-horse and you'd say *it* was beautiful! On my life—and I don't say this to praise myself—but I'm as beautiful as your Melibea!

AREUSA. Even so, sister, you haven't seen her as I have. As God is my witness, if you could see her without her makeup on you'd be so sick at your stomach you'd not be able to eat all day! She stays indoors a year on end all covered with plasters made out of every kind of filth. When she goes out where she can be seen even once she bedaubs her face with gall and honey and other things I won't mention because we're at the table. It's their money that makes them beautiful and admired, not the graces of their bodies. For a virgin, her breasts, upon my word, look as though she'd had three children! They're as big as melons! I haven't seen her belly, but to judge by the rest of her it must be as flabby as if she were fifty! I can't imagine what ails Calisto that makes him turn away from other girls he could have more easily and who'd give him a better time!

SEMPRONIO. It strikes me that each of you peddlers is hawking her own wares. In the city they say the contrary.

AREUSA. Nothing is less to be trusted than vulgar opinion. You'll never be happy if you go by what people say. Whatever the mob thinks is nonsense; what it reproves is goodness; what it approves is wickedness. So don't take seriously what people say about the loveliness and beauty of Melibea.

SEMPRONIO. The people, dear mistress, don't usually spare the faults of their betters, so I don't think they'd have neglected

Melibea's, if she's got any. But, even allowing that what you say is true, Calisto's a gentleman and Melibea's a lady, and they naturally prefer those born in their own class. So there's nothing astonishing in his loving her rather than one of you.

AREUSA. If the coat fits him let him wear it! Deeds are what make nobility. We're all children of Adam and Eve. Let every man be judged by his works and not go around riding on the skirts of his ancestors!

CELESTINA. Children, if you love me stop your bickering. And you, Elicia, come back to the table and quit pouting.

ELICIA. If I sat down again I'd vomit! How can I sit next to that scum who tells me to my face that that ragbag of a Melibea is prettier than I am!

SEMPRONIO. Hush, my dear. You made the comparison yourself. All comparisons are odious. The fault is yours.

AREUSA. Come back to the table, sister. Don't give these pigheaded fools that satisfaction. If you won't sit down I'll leave the table myself.

ELICIA. Well, I'll do it only to please you and be polite, not to satisfy him!

SEMPRONIO. He, he, he!

ELICIA. What are you laughing about? I hope that nasty mouth of yours gets eaten by a cancer!

CELESTINA. Don't answer her, son. If you do we'll never finish. . . . Tell me, how is Calisto? How did you leave him? How were you two able to give him the slip?

PARMENO. He ran off like mad to the Magdalene, cursing and breathing fire, desperate and half crazy, to pray God to give you strength to gnaw the bones of these chickens, and swearing he wouldn't go home until he heard you had Melibea in your skirt. Your cloak and cape are as good as won, and even my coat! I'm not so certain about the money; I don't know when he'll pay you.

CELESTINA. It doesn't matter. It will be just as welcome whenever we get it. You're always glad to get something if you don't have to work too hard for it, especially from such a rich man, so rich that I could leave this beggary behind with the leftovers from his table, he's got so much. It doesn't hurt the rich to spend their money in a good cause. And if they're addled with love they don't feel any pain at parting with it, for they're deaf and dumb. I learned this from others who weren't as sick as he is. They can't eat or drink, laugh or cry, sleep or stay awake, speak or keep silent, suffer or rest from suffering. They're neither contented nor discontented, so complicated is this ulcer of theirs! They're so absent-minded that when they eat, their hands stop half way to their mouths. If you speak to them they can't answer sensibly. It's the same with their bodies: their hearts and senses are with their mistresses. Love is so strong that it not only crosses the land, but even the seas. It has the same authority with every kind of men. It breaks through all barriers; it is anxious, fearful, and cautious; it looks around in all directions. You true lovers judge whether I'm talking nonsense or not!

SEMPRONIO. Mistress, I agree with you entirely, for this little one here made me go about for a time like another Calisto, out of my head, tired, vacant, sleeping poorly by day and not at all by night, writing bad verses, making faces, jumping over walls, risking my life daily, running bulls, racing horses, breaking swords, building ladders, tossing the bar, throwing the javelin, wearing armor, boring my friends, and doing the thousand and one silly things that mad lovers do. But it was worth it! I won a jewel!

ELICIA. So you think you've got me safe, do you? If you weren't blind you'd see another man in the house I love better, smarter than you, who doesn't go around looking for some way to annoy me! You come to see me only once a year, and then you get here late and for no good purpose!

CELESTINA. Let her rave, son. The more she talks like that the more it proves she loves you. It's all because you praised Melibea, and she can't think of any other way of getting back at you. She doesn't know whether she's had her dinner or not. And this

cousin of hers, well, I know what she is like, too! Enjoy yourselves while you're young, for whoever gets a chance to do so but
waits for a better one will regret it, just as I regret the few hours
I wasted when I was a girl and had admirers and lovers. Sinner
that I am, I'm in my dotage now and no one loves me! But God
knows I'd like it! So kiss and make up and I'll enjoy watching
you, which is the only pleasure I've got left. At the table everything from the waist up is allowable, but when you leave it I
won't make any conditions, since the law doesn't. I know from
my girls that you lads will never be accused of disappointing
them, and old Celestina will mumble the crumbs that fall from
your table. God bless you! How good it is to see you play, you
little buggers! You rascals! That's the way these little spats
should end! Watch out! Don't upset the table!

ELICIA. Mother, someone's knocking at the door! Our cake is
dough!

CELESTINA. Go and see who it is, daughter. Maybe it's someone
who'll join in.

ELICIA. Unless I'm mistaken, it's my cousin Lucrecia's voice.

CELESTINA. Open the door and bring her in! This is our lucky
year! She's got an interest in this business of ours, even if they
do keep her so shut in that she can't have any fun.

AREUSA. That's a fact! These poor girls who work for great ladies
never do. They never learn anything about love. That's why I've
been on my own ever since I got good sense. I never wanted to
belong to anyone but myself. And that goes especially for these
fine ladies nowadays. You waste the best part of your life working for them, and they pay you with a ragged cast-off skirt for
ten years of service! They do nothing but insult you and scold
you and keep you down, and you don't dare open your mouth in
front of them. And when they see it's getting time to marry you
off, they start the rumor that you're sleeping with the flunkey
or with their son, or you're having an affair with their husband,
or you're bringing men into the house, or you stole a cup or lost

a ring. They beat you black and blue and then throw you out the door with your skirt over your head and scream: "Get out of here, you thief, you whore! You're not going to stay here and ruin my house and reputation!" So instead of a reward you get insulted; you expect to get a husband and you get left; you expect wedding presents and clothes, but they throw you out naked and jeered at! That's the way they pay you! Don't ever expect them to call you by your right name, only: "Come here, you whore! Go there, you slut! Where are you going, you rascal? Why did you do this, you dirty tramp? Did you eat that, you glutton? Look how you cleaned the frying pan, you pig! Why didn't you wash the tablecloth, you sloven? Did you lose that plate, you careless fool? What became of the towel, you thief? You must have given it to that ruffian of yours! Come here, you wicked girl! Where's that cold chicken? Go find it at once! If you don't, I'll take it out of your wages!" And along with this, it's nothing but blows with their slippers, and pinching and beating and whipping from morning till night! You can never please them. They love to scream at you and scolding is their delight. They're least pleased with what you do best. And that's why, mother, I chose to live in my little house by myself, owing nothing to anyone, my own mistress, rather than live a prisoner in a palace.

CELESTINA. Your head is screwed on right. The wise man said: "Better a crust in peace than a full house with strife." But enough of that. Here's Lucrecia.

LUCRECIA. A good appetite to you, aunt and company! God bless such honest people! And so many of you!

CELESTINA. So many, daughter? Do you think this is many? You didn't know me in my good days. How different things are now! It's enough to break your heart! I've seen, my dear, at this very table where your cousins are sitting, nine girls of your age. The oldest wasn't more than nineteen, the youngest not less than fourteen. That's the way the world goes! Let it go! Fortune turns her wheel, bringing up her cups, some full, some empty. It's her law that nothing shall stay the same for long; her law is change. It would make me weep to tell you how respected I was in those days and how I've come down since, for my sins and bad luck! As the old proverb has it: everything in this world either grows or shrinks. Everything has its limits and its ups and downs. My renown reached its height along with my person; it had to decline—which makes me think I haven't got much longer to live.

LUCRECIA. You must have had plenty of work, mother, with all those girls to manage. That's not the easiest kind of flock to guard!

CELESTINA. Work, my dear? Not so! It was a solace and a comfort! They all obeyed me; they all honored and respected me; none of them ever lost my love. My word was law. I gave to each what she earned. They accepted only those I told them to accept: lame, or one-eyed, or one-armed. They considered him best who paid me most. The profit was mine, the work theirs. They brought me plenty of customers: old gentlemen and young, and clergymen of all ranks, from bishops to sextons. Why, the moment I entered a church hats would come off in my honor as if I were a duchess! The one who had the least traffic with me considered himself the meanest. When they saw me half a league off they'd leave their prayers, and one by one and two by two they'd come running to greet me and ask whether there wasn't some little thing they could do for me, and each would ask me about his girl. Some, even while they were saying Mass, seeing me come in, would get so flustered that they'd say everything wrong. Some called me "mistress"; others, "aunt"; others, "sweetheart"; others, "honest old woman." There they arranged their visits to my house, and mine to theirs. There they'd offer me money, or gifts, or they'd kiss the hem of my shawl or my cheek, to keep me happy. But now my fortune has reached such an ebb that you may well say: "I hope your shoes hold out!"

SEMPRONIO. We're amazed at what you tell us of those pious people and saintly tonsures. Surely they couldn't all have been like that!

CELESTINA. No, my son, and God forbid I should repeat such a slander! There were many pious *old* men with whom I made no headway. Some of them couldn't stand the sight of me, but I rather think it was from envy of the others. The clergy were so numerous that there were some of all kinds: some very chaste, and others whose duty it was to support me in my profession. There are still some of these, I think. They used to send their squires and servants to escort me home, and I had hardly got there when quantities of chickens, geese, ducks, partridges, pigeons, hams, wheat cakes, and sucking pigs would come pouring in at the door! As soon as they received their share of the holy tithes they ran to enter it in my book so that I and their sweethearts could eat. And wine? I had plenty and to spare of the best that was drunk in the city: Monviedro, Toro, Madrigal, San Martín, and wines from many other cellars, too numerous for me to remember, although I can still taste them. It's too much to expect of an old woman like me, that she should tell you the origin of a wine merely from smelling it. And there were some poor priests without benefices who brought me votive offerings from the altars. As soon as their last parishioners had kissed their stoles, they were off to my house with the first flight. Crowds of boys used to come to my door loaded down with provisions. . . . I don't know how I stand it now after having been so rich!

AREUSA. For goodness' sake, mother, we came here to have a good time! Don't cry and carry on so! God will take care of you.

CELESTINA. I've got plenty to cry about, remembering the happy times and the good life I had, and how I was waited upon by everybody! If a new kind of fruit appeared I was the first to taste it. They had to come to my house for it if they wanted it for some pregnant woman.

SEMPRONIO. There's no use mourning over the good old days if you can't get them back. It just makes you sad and you spoil our fun crying over them. Clear the table. We'll go upstairs and amuse ourselves while you find out what this girl wants.

CELESTINA. All that aside, tell me, daughter Lucrecia, what you came for.

LUCRECIA. To tell the truth, mother, listening to you talk about those gay times, I'd quite forgotten my errand. I could listen to you for a year without eating! What a good life those girls had! I can see myself in their place. . . . You must know the reason of my visit, mother. My mistress wants her girdle back and she begs you to come and see her very soon, because she feels faint and ill and has got a pain in her heart.

CELESTINA. Daughter, little pains like that are more noise than substance. I'm surprised that such a young woman should have anything wrong with her heart.

LUCRECIA. *I hope they drag you through the streets, you old traitor! So you don't know what's the matter with Melibea? This false old witch casts her spell and leaves, and then she's surprised!*

CELESTINA. What are you saying, daughter?

LUCRECIA. That we should hurry, mother, and that you should give me the girdle.

CELESTINA. Come! I'll bring it myself.

ACT X

Pleberio's house.   Melibea, Celestina,
Lucrecia, Alisa.

MELIBEA. Alas, poor fool! Poor silly girl that I was! How much
better it would have been to yield to Celestina yesterday, when
she came to plead for that gentleman who so charmed me! How
much better to have made him happy as well as myself than
to have to reveal my true feeling when, perhaps, he won't thank
me for it! When, perhaps, despairing of a fair answer, he will
have set his eyes upon another! Oh, my faithful Lucrecia, what
will you say? What will you think of me? How dismayed you
will be at my loss of shame and modesty, which I once guarded
as a sheltered maiden should! Do you suspect, I wonder, the
source of my affliction? Oh, if you'd only come and bring my
blessed mediator with you!

Almighty God, Thou whom those in trouble call upon; Thou
to whom the wretched go for comfort and the stricken for relief;
Thou whom heaven and earth obey, and the regions under the
earth; Thou who mad'st all things subject to man, humbly I beseech Thee to arm my heart with patience, that I may hide my
fearful sickness and tarnish not the shield of chastity I have laid
upon my love, lest I discover the true cause of the pain that tortures me!

But how is this to be, so cruelly am I hurt by the poisoned
sweet I tasted at the sight of Calisto? Oh woman, woman, timid
and frail! Why is it not given to us to reveal our galling and
burning love, as it is to man? Ah, then Calisto would be happy
and I free of this misery!

LUCRECIA. Wait at the door, aunt, while I go up and see who my mistress is talking to. . . . Come up, come up! She's talking to herself.

MELIBEA. Draw the screen, Lucrecia. Oh wise and honest old woman, you're welcome! You didn't imagine I'd need your skill so soon, or that I'd be begging you for a favor as you once begged me.

CELESTINA. What trouble is this, my lady, that has so driven the color from your face?

MELIBEA. Oh mother, my breast is full of serpents!

CELESTINA. *Good! That's just what I wanted! You're going to pay me, my mistress, for your bad temper!*

MELIBEA. What are you saying? Does the source of my sickness show in my face?

CELESTINA. You haven't told me yet what your trouble is, my lady. Do you expect me to divine it? I was saying that it makes me sad to see your lovely face so overcast with gloom.

MELIBEA. Honest old woman, do you make it more cheerful, for I've heard great things of your knowledge.

CELESTINA. The only one who knows, my lady, is God; but, since He gave of His knowledge to men that they might discover medicines and heal the sick, either by experience, art, or natural instinct, some small part of it fell to the lot of this poor old woman who's at your service.

MELIBEA. How comforting it is to hear you! The visitor's cheerful face is good medicine for the patient. My heart, it seems to me, lies in pieces in your hands. Do you, with the power of your words, make it whole again. For the love of God take off your cloak and diagnose my sickness and cure me!

CELESTINA. The most effective part of a cure is for the patient to desire it, so I don't think your malady can be dangerous. But if, with the help of God, I'm to prescribe the proper treatment,

I must know three things: First, in what part of your body do you feel the greatest pain? Second, is your sickness recent? For diseases are more readily cured at their beginning than when they've become chronic; animals are tamed more quickly when they're young, and they obey more willingly, than when their hides have grown tough; plants grow better if they're set out while new and tender than while in fruit; and a new sin is more easily got rid of than one we commit every day from ancient habit. Third, does your trouble arise from some painful thought hidden in your mind? When I know these things you'll see my treatment take effect. It's as necessary, therefore, to speak truthfully to your physician as it is to your confessor.

MELIBEA. Friend Celestina, my wise and skillful doctor, you make it possible for me to open my heart to you, for you speak like a woman expert in treating such diseases. My pain is in my heart, under the left breast, but it sends its pangs to all parts of my body. I never thought a pain could be so sharp as to drive me out of my senses, as this one does! It takes the color from my face and destroys my appetite; I cannot sleep, nor can I bear to hear any kind of merriment. Finally, if it was caused by some secret thought, I can't think what that thought could have been: not the death of a dear one, or the loss of my worldly goods, or a terrifying vision, or some wild nightmare. The only thing it could have been was the tumult you stirred up in me with your suspicious request in behalf of that gentleman, Calisto, when you asked for the prayer.

CELESTINA. What, my lady? Is he then such a wicked man? Is his name so horrid that the mere mention of it is poison to you? Don't believe it! That's not the cause of your trouble, but another, I suspect. If I'm correct, my lady, and if you'll give me leave to speak, I'll tell you what it is.

MELIBEA. What is this, Celestina? Do you need my permission to heal me? What physician ever asked leave to treat his patient? Speak! Speak! You always have my permission if my honor is safe.

CELESTINA. My lady, you're torn between worry over your sickness and your dread of the treatment. Your fear makes me afraid, my fear makes me silent, and if I can't speak I can't treat you.

MELIBEA. The longer you put it off the more you increase my suffering. Either you know nothing, or your physic is compounded of the poison of infamy and the liquor of corruption, with an admixture of pain on the part of the patient. If neither of these considerations prevents you, you have my leave to give me any medicine whatever, provided my honor is safe. I beg you to bring it out!

CELESTINA. It's not surprising, my lady, that the wounded man suffers more acutely from the burning turpentine and the surgeon's rough stitches than he did when he first received the wound in his healthy flesh. If you wish to be well, and if you can bear to watch the sharp point of my fine needle without flinching, bind your hands and feet with the bandage of calm, your eyes with reverence, your tongue with silence, stop your ears with the cotton of patience, and watch your old mistress work!

MELIBEA. You drive me frantic with your rambling! For God's sake, say whatever you like and do whatever you can! Whatever it is, it cannot be as painful as my torment! Attack my honor, destroy my reputation, spoil my body, tear open my breast, and remove my heart! Whatever you do, you'll be safe and well paid for it, if you bring me relief!

LUCRECIA. *My mistress is beside herself! What great evil is this? She's in the old witch's power!*

CELESTINA. *There's always some devil about! I escape from Parmeno and stumble over Lucrecia!*

MELIBEA. What are you saying, mother? What did Lucrecia say?

CELESTINA. I didn't hear her say anything; but for a proper cure I can't have anyone present, so please ask her to leave. Forgive me, daughter Lucrecia!

MELIBEA. Leave us, Lucrecia. Quickly now!

LUCRECIA. *Ah yes, she's lost!* I'm going, my lady.

CELESTINA. Your suffering emboldens me to prescribe for you. Besides, you've already taken part of my physic. But you must let me bring you a better and more comforting medicine from Calisto's house.

MELIBEA. Hush, mother, in God's name! Don't bring anything from his house and don't mention his name in this one.

CELESTINA. You must have patience, my lady, to suffer the sting of the first stitch, which is the most important one. Don't break it, for if you do all our work will be wasted. You've got a deep wound and it needs severe treatment. What is hard is soonest softened by something that is also hard. The learned say that a cure made by a soft-hearted surgeon leaves a bigger scar, and that a danger is never met without danger. One nail is driven out with another, one pain with another. You must be patient, for a troublesome disease can rarely be cured without trouble. Don't hate so virtuous a person as Calisto, nor allow your tongue to speak ill of him, for if it should come to his ears. . . .

MELIBEA. My God, you're killing me! Haven't I told you not to praise that man in my presence, or even speak of him?

CELESTINA. That's the second stitch, my lady. If you refuse it in your impatience my visit will do you little good. If, on the other hand, you take it as you promised, you'll be well and out of debt, and Calisto will be happy and well paid. But you cry before you feel the prick of my fine needle, merely at the mention of it!

MELIBEA. You've brought him up so many times that I won't stand it, no matter how many promises or permissions I gave you! How will he be paid? What do I owe him? In what way am I in his debt? What has he ever done for me? Why is he necessary in my treatment? When you mention his name it's as if you were tearing my heart out of my body!

CELESTINA. Love found its way into your heart without even tearing your clothes, and I'll not have to tear them to cure you.

MELIBEA. What do they call this sickness of mine that has so penetrated into every part of my being?

CELESTINA. It's called sweet love.

MELIBEA. Is it so? It makes me happy merely to hear it!

CELESTINA. Love is a hidden fire, a pleasant canker, a savory poison, a sweet bitterness, a delightful distress, a joyous torture, a grateful and cruel wound, a gentle death.

MELIBEA. Alas, poor wretch that I am! If what you say is true, my recovery is doubtful. Your words are full of contradictions.

CELESTINA. Let not your noble youth, my lady, despair of health. When God sends a disease He also sends a remedy for it, which is especially true of yours, for I know of a flower now in bloom that will cure you quite.

MELIBEA. What's it called?

CELESTINA. I hardly dare name it.

MELIBEA. Tell me; don't be afraid.

CELESTINA. It's called Calisto. . . . Oh my goodness, my lady Melibea! What is this? She has fainted! Oh miserable fool that I am! Let me raise her head. Oh luckless old woman! Was this how my life was to end? If she dies they'll kill me! And even if she lives I'll be found out, for she can hardly help talking about her sickness and my treatment of it. . . . My lady Melibea, my angel, what ails you? Can't you speak to me, my sweet? You're so pale! Open your lovely eyes! Lucrecia! Lucrecia! Come quickly! Your mistress has fainted in my arms! Run down and get a pitcher of water!

MELIBEA. Wait! I'm better now. Don't stir up the house.

CELESTINA. Oh what have I done? Don't faint again, my lady! Speak to me as you used.

MELIBEA. I'll speak much better than I used. Hush now. Don't weary me further.

CELESTINA. But what do you want me to do, my lovely pearl? What was that seizure of yours? I think my stitches are giving way.

MELIBEA. What is giving way is my honesty and my shame, which, because they were so much a part of me, took with them for a space my color, my strength, my tongue, and a good part of my senses. Oh my good doctor, my faithful friend, it would be vain for me to try to conceal what you can now so plainly see! When that noble gentleman spoke to me of love some days ago, his words troubled me, but now that you've named him, I find them full of joy. Your stitches have closed my wound and I love you for it! You bound me with my girdle and made me his prisoner. His toothache became my sharpest torment, his pain my greatest pain. How can I thank you for your patience, your wise audacity, your abundant skill, your firmness, your solicitous and faithful steps, your pleasant words, and your great anxiety for me? Calisto is in your debt, and I even more. No matter how I reproached you, you did not slacken your efforts, nor did you doubt yourself or the wisdom of your course. On the contrary, like a faithful servant, the more I abused you, the more diligent you were; the more I mistreated you, the greater effort you made; the more harshly I spoke, the more smiling was your face; the angrier I became, the more humble you were. Putting aside all fear, you extracted from my breast what I never meant to show you or anyone else.

CELESTINA. It wasn't such a great thing I did, my friend and lady mistress, for my good purpose gives me courage to brave the scoldings of protected maidens like yourself. While I was on my way here, to be sure, and even afterward, I hesitated to tell you of my errand. I feared your father's power, but Calisto's gentleness made me bold. Your caution made me cautious, but your goodness and kindness encouraged me. I wavered between fear and duty. But now that you've revealed this great matter, my lady, speak your will, pour your secrets into my lap, and leave the rest to me. I promise that you and Calisto will see your desires fulfilled.

MELIBEA. Oh Calisto, my dear lord! My sweet and gentle love! If your heart feels what mine does now, how can you bear to live apart from me? Oh my mother and mistress, do you contrive to let me see him soon, if you love me!

CELESTINA. You'll see him and speak with him as well.

MELIBEA. Speak with him? Impossible!

CELESTINA. Nothing is impossible to those who will.

MELIBEA. Tell me how.

CELESTINA. I've thought of it: at your door.

MELIBEA. If you can do that I'll worship you! At what hour?

CELESTINA. At midnight.

MELIBEA. Go then, my mistress, my loyal friend! See him and tell him to come quietly. At my door, then, at midnight, and we'll arrange things to his liking!

CELESTINA. Good-bye now. Your mother's coming.

MELIBEA. Lucrecia, my friend and faithful confidante, you see, don't you, that I couldn't help myself? I am that gentleman's prisoner. I beseech you, in God's name, to lock my secret in your heart so I may delight in my gentle love! If you do so I'll hold you as dear as your true service deserves.

LUCRECIA. Since you had to choose between living and dying, you were right to choose the better course.

ALISA. What brings you here so frequently, neighbor?

CELESTINA. My lady, the thread I sold you yesterday was a little short in weight, and I came to make it good, as I promised. I brought it and now I'm leaving. God be with you!

ALISA. And may He go with you!

ALISA. Daughter Melibea, what did the old woman want?

MELIBEA. She came to sell a bit of whiting.

ALISA. I can believe that more easily than what the old rascal told me. She lied because she thought I wouldn't like her coming here. Watch her, daughter! She's a tricky one! The clever thief always hangs about the houses of the rich. This one, with her wiles, will corrupt good manners.

LUCRECIA. *You thought of that too late, mistress!*

ALISA. As you love me, daughter, if she comes again and I don't see her, don't bid her welcome or receive her pleasantly. When she hears your honest answer she'll not return, for virtue is more to be feared than a sword.

MELIBEA. Is she one of those? I'll not see her again. I'm glad you told me about her, my lady, and I'll be on my guard.

ACT XI

SCENE 1. *The Magdalene. Later, a street. Celestina, Calisto, Parmeno, Sempronio.*

CELESTINA. Oh Lord, I can hardly stagger under such a load of joy! There go Parmeno and Sempronio into the Magdalene. I'll follow them. If Calisto isn't there we'll go to his house and demand our reward for bringing good news.

SEMPRONIO. Look, sir, you've been here so long that people are beginning to notice it. Don't get yourself talked about. They call an overly devout man a hypocrite. They'll say you go around kissing saints. When you're sick you ought to stay at home, not spread it abroad. Don't show strangers your troubles. After all, the tambourine is in the hands of one who knows how to play it.

CALISTO. In whose hands?

SEMPRONIO. Celestina's.

CELESTINA. Who said Celestina? What are you saying about this slave of Calisto's? I've been hurrying to overtake you all along Archdeacon Street, but these long skirts get in my way.

CALISTO. Oh my jewel! My refuge! You're never out of my thoughts! It gladdens my heart to see your honest face, your noble old age. Tell me, what word do you bring that makes you so happy? What life-saving tidings have you got for me? What does my life depend upon?

CELESTINA. My tongue.

CALISTO. What do you say, my glory and my comfort? Explain yourself.

CELESTINA. Let's leave the church, sir, and on the way to your house I'll tell you something that will make you happy indeed!

PARMENO. The old woman's in high spirits, brother. She must be bringing some good news.

SEMPRONIO. Listen to her.

CELESTINA. I've spent the whole day, sir, working for you, while I neglected others, which will cost me a pretty penny. I make you happy, but others complain of me. I've lost more than you think. But it's well spent, for I've got great news for you. I bring you greetings from Melibea! She's yours!

CALISTO. What do I hear?

CELESTINA. That she belongs to you more than to herself! She'll obey you sooner than her father Pleberio!

CALISTO. Softly, mother! Don't say such things! These lads will be saying you're crazy. Melibea's my sovereign! Melibea's my life! Melibea's my God! I'm her captive and her slave!

SEMPRONIO. You have too little confidence in yourself, sir. You so depreciate and scorn yourself that you won't let Celestina finish her report. You upset us all with such nonsense. Why are you crossing yourself? Give her something for her trouble. She's earned it!

CALISTO. You're right! My dear mother, I know that my poor gift can never requite you for your pains. Take this little chain instead of the cloak and skirt I promised you. And now go on with your wonderful story!

PARMENO. He called it a *little* chain! You heard him, Sempronio. He doesn't care how much he spends. I wouldn't sell my share of it for half a mark of gold, no matter how unfairly the old woman divides it!

SEMPRONIO. Our master will hear you! We'll have to calm him down and cure you of babbling. You're always complaining. If you love me, brother, listen and shut up! That's why God gave you two ears and only one mouth.

PARMENO. Let the devil listen to her! Calisto's hanging on the old crone's words as if he were struck deaf, dumb, and blind! He's so besotted that if we thumbed our noses at him he'd think we were praying God to give him success!

SEMPRONIO. Silence! Listen carefully to Celestina. By my soul, she has earned whatever he gives her and more! Oh what she's telling him!

CELESTINA. My lord Calisto, you're too generous to this weak old woman. A favor or a gift is to be judged great or small according to the giver of it, so I don't give too much importance to my not deserving it. It's too rich and grand for me, but, measured against your magnificence, it's nothing. I've earned it by restoring your health, which was ruined; your heart, which was missing; your wits, which were clouded. Melibea longs for you more than you long for her. Melibea loves you and yearns to see you. Melibea spends more time thinking of your looks than she does of her own. Melibea says she's yours and considers that her title to liberty, and with it she quiets the fire that's consuming her more than it does you.

CALISTO. Am I really here, my lads? My lads, do I hear aright? See whether I'm awake, my lads! Is it day or night? Lord God in heaven, don't let this turn out to be a dream! I'm awake! If you're making this up, mistress, just to please me, don't be afraid, but tell me the truth. You deserve what I gave you for your efforts alone.

CELESTINA. Never did a loving heart believe good tidings or doubt bad ones. But you'll see whether I'm joking or not if you'll go to her house tonight at the stroke of twelve, as I arranged with her, and talk with her at her door. She'll tell you at greater length how busy I've been, how much she longs for you and loves you, and who brought it all to pass.

CALISTO. Could I hope for such a thing? Could something like this happen to *me*? I'll die between here and there! I can't contain so much happiness! How can I deserve such a gift? How can I be worthy to speak with such a lady? And at her request!

CELESTINA. I've always heard that good fortune is harder to bear than bad, for good fortune doesn't bring tranquillity and bad fortune does bring consolation. Why not consider your own worth, my lord Calisto? Why not take credit for the time you've spent in her service? Why not take into account the person you've got for an intermediary? Also, that until now you've always doubted you could succeed, and how patient you've been? And now that I tell you your pain is over, you would end your life? Remember, Celestina is with you! Even though you lacked everything a lover should have, she'd pass you off for the most accomplished gallant in the world! She'd level mountains to make your way easier, and tame the raging torrents so you could cross them dry-shod. You don't know this old woman!

CALISTO. See here, mistress, what are you saying? That she will come to the door of her own free will?

CELESTINA. And even on her knees!

SEMPRONIO. Unless this is some witch's trap to catch us all! Look, mother, they conceal poison in bread so the rats won't taste it.

PARMENO. You never said a truer word! That lady's sudden yielding and her over-prompt love for Celestina strike me as very odd. It looks as though she may be hoodwinking us like a gypsy with her sweet and ready talk, the better to catch us off guard.

CALISTO. Shut up, you fools, you suspicious rascals! Are you trying to make me believe that angels can do wrong? For Melibea is an angel in disguise living among us!

SEMPRONIO. Back to his heresies again! Listen to him, Parmeno! But don't let it worry you. If this is a trick he'll pay for it. We've got good legs!

CELESTINA. You're right, sir. They're full of idle suspicions. Well, I've done everything you asked me to do. I've made you happy. Now may God free you and make you well! I leave you very contentedly. If you need me further for this or for anything else, I'm at your service.

PARMENO. He, he, he!

SEMPRONIO. What's so funny, Parmeno?

PARMENO. Look what a hurry the old devil is in! She can't wait to sell the chain. She can't believe it's hers or that he really gave it to her. She doesn't deserve such a reward, any more than Calisto deserves Melibea!

SEMPRONIO. What did you expect of an old whore whose ordinary price for mending maidenheads is seven for a tuppence? She's afraid they'll take it away from her. But she'd better watch herself when she divides it up, or we'll take care of *her!*

CALISTO. Go with God, mother! I want to sleep and rest a while to make up for past nights and get ready for this one.

SCENE 2.   *Celestina's house.*
Celestina, Elicia.

CELESTINA. (Knocks.)

ELICIA. Who's there?

CELESTINA. Open up, daughter Elicia!

ELICIA. What kept you so late? You shouldn't stay out like this, you're too old! You'll stumble over something and fall and kill yourself.

CELESTINA. I'm not afraid of that. I plot by day the course I'm going to sail by night. But that isn't what's worrying you.

ELICIA. Well, what *is* worrying me?

CELESTINA. Your guest walked out on you.

ELICIA. But that was four hours ago! Why should I be worrying about that?

CELESTINA. The sooner they leave the worse you feel, quite properly. But never mind your being left in the lurch and my being late. Let's have a bite to eat and then to bed.

ACT XII

SCENE 1. *Calisto's house. Calisto, Sempronio, Parmeno.*

CALISTO. What time is it, my lads?

SEMPRONIO. It just struck ten.

CALISTO. You careless rascal! How is it, fool, that, knowing what I've got at stake, you say the first thing that pops into your head? If I'd been asleep and had depended on you, and you had made ten out of eleven, or eleven out of ten, and Melibea had come to her door and I wasn't there, she'd have gone back in and I'd have been cheated. It's certainly true, what they say, that other folks' troubles are the easiest to bear!

SEMPRONIO. It seems to me, sir, to be as wrong to ask a question when you know the answer as it is to reply without knowing it. *This master of mine is trying to pick a quarrel and doesn't know where to begin.*

PARMENO. It would be better, sir, to spend this last hour in arming ourselves rather than in fault-finding.

CALISTO. Fetch me my armor, Parmeno.

PARMENO. Here it is, sir.

CALISTO. Help me on with it. Take a look outside, Sempronio, and see whether anyone's in the street.

SEMPRONIO. There's no one, sir, and, even if there were, it's so dark you'd not be recognized.

SCENE 2.   *Pleberio's house.   Calisto,*
Sempronio, Parmeno; Melibea,
Lucrecia, Pleberio, Alisa.

CALISTO. Let's go this way; it's longer but safer. It's striking twelve. A good hour!

PARMENO. We're almost there.

CALISTO. We're on time. Go up to the house, Parmeno, and see if my lady is at her door.

PARMENO. I, sir? God forbid I should meddle in another's affair! You'd better show yourself first. If she sees me she'll be frightened to think her secret is known by so many. Or perhaps she'll think you've jilted her.

CALISTO. You're right, Parmeno! Your good advice has saved me. I'd have died if she had gone back in through my stupidity. I'll go up; you two stay here.

PARMENO. What do you think of that, Sempronio? Our fool master thought he could hide behind me if things went wrong. How do I know who's hiding behind that door? There may be treachery afoot. How do I know Melibea isn't getting ready to pay him off for his insolence? We don't even know the old woman was telling the truth. *Don't talk, Parmeno! You'll get killed and you won't know who did it! Don't be a flatterer, as your master wants you to be, and you'll never be crying over other people's troubles! Don't take Celestina's advice and get left in the lurch! Go offer your advice and honest opinions and get a beating for your pains! Keep on the way you were going and end up in the street! It seems to me I've just begun to live, I've escaped from such a trap!*

SEMPRONIO. Quiet, Parmeno! Don't make all that racket just because you're feeling good. They'll hear you.

PARMENO. Hush, brother! It's too good to be true! Why, I got him to believe I was doing him a favor by not going to the door, when I was merely looking out for my own interests! Did anyone ever do so well for himself? But from now on, if you'll keep your eye on me, you'll see me do things to Calisto and everyone who's mixed up in this affair of his! I'm certain that that girl is a bait he'll get himself hooked on, or meat for a buzzard trap, and he'll be sorry if he eats it!

SEMPRONIO. Come! Don't worry your head with such suspicions, even if they turn out to be correct. On your mark! At the first shout you hear, take to your heels!

PARMENO. Brother, we studied out of the same textbook! I'm wearing light breeches and leggings for that very reason. I'm glad you brought it up; I was ashamed to. If our master's caught, I don't think he can escape from Pleberio's men, and in that case he won't be able to call us to account afterward and accuse us of running away.

SEMPRONIO. Oh my friend Parmeno, how good it is to have a companion to share one's thoughts! Even if Celestina did nothing else for us, this would be enough.

PARMENO. You're right! It's plain that if we stood by him just because we were afraid of each other and afraid of being accused of cowardice, we'd get killed along with him, and he isn't worth it.

SEMPRONIO. Melibea must be there. Listen! They're talking low.

PARMENO. I wonder if it's Melibea, or someone who's imitating her voice.

SEMPRONIO. God deliver us from traitors! I hope they haven't blocked off the street. That's the only thing that worries me.

CALISTO. There's more than one person in there! But I'll speak, no matter who it is. Mistress?

LUCRECIA. That's Calisto's voice. I'll go see. . . . Who is it? Who's there?

CALISTO. He who obeys your summons.

LUCRECIA. Why don't you come to the door, mistress? It's that gentleman!

MELIBEA. Quiet, you fool! Make sure!

LUCRECIA. Come, mistress, it is he! I recognize his voice.

CALISTO. This is a trick! That isn't Melibea's voice! I hear a noise! I'm betrayed! But I'll not stir from this spot, dead or alive!

MELIBEA. Lucrecia, do you go back to bed for a little. . . . Sir, who are you? Who asked you to come here?

CALISTO. I was commanded to come by one who deserves to command the whole world! By one I'm not worthy to serve! Don't be afraid to show yourself to your prisoner. The sound of your sweet voice, which is never absent from my ears, tells me you're my mistress Melibea. I'm your servant Calisto.

MELIBEA. The great audacity of your messages, my lord Calisto, has forced me to speak with you. You had my reply to your first one, and I don't know what else you can expect from me. Put by your vain and foolish enterprise, or my honor and person will fall under some evil suspicion. That's why I'm here, to bid you farewell and find peace. Don't make my name a sport for wagging tongues.

CALISTO. Oh unfortunate Calisto, how your servants have cheated you! Oh deceitful Celestina, why did you falsify the words of my mistress? Why did you use your tongue to destroy me? What purpose did you have in sending me here, save to confront me with the antipathy, the refusal, the distrust, the hatred, of her who holds the keys to my damnation or my glory? You're my enemy! Didn't you assure me that she had commanded me of her own free will to come to this place, and that she had ordered my banishment to be lifted? Whom can I trust? Where can I find the truth? Who is an open enemy? Who a true friend? Where is treachery not found? Who is it that dared to plant this cruel hope in me?

MELIBEA. Cease, my lord, your just complaints. My heart cannot bear it, nor can my eyes conceal their pity. You are sad and you weep because you believe me cruel; I weep from pleasure at seeing you so constant. Oh my dear lord and all my happiness! How much sweeter would it be to see your face than to hear your voice! But we can do nothing further now, so believe the true words I sent you by our faithful messenger. I confirm and approve everything she told you. Dry your eyes, sir, and command me as you please.

CALISTO. Oh my mistress, my hope of glory, comfort and relief of my pain, joy of my heart! Where shall I find words to thank you for the ineffable gift you have given me in this moment of my anguish, to allow this weak and unworthy one to enjoy your sweet love? When I saw your high estate, your perfection, your nobility, and compared my unworthiness with your great worth, with your limitless graces, and your manifest and justly celebrated virtues, I felt myself undeserving of you. Oh high God, how can I thank Thee for the wonders Thou has wrought for me! I banished this thought from my heart as impossible long days ago, until the bright beams of your shining countenance gave light to my eyes, warmth to my heart, and voice to my tongue; increased my self-respect, vanquished my faint-heartedness, overcame my diffidence, doubled my strength, thawed the numbness from my feet and hands, and, finally, filled me with such courage that I now find myself in ecstasy listening to your sweet voice! Had I not known its health-giving fragrance, I could not have believed your words to be free of deception, but now that I am certain of your pure intentions I am wondering whether I am really this Calisto for whom such glorious things have been done!

MELIBEA. Ever since I learned who you were, my lord Calisto, and your high worth, your great gifts and exalted birth, you have been in my heart at every moment. I strove for some days to hide it from myself, but when that woman mentioned your sweet name to me I could no longer conceal my feeling, nor could I forbear coming here to you. And now I beg you to dispose of my person as you will. I curse these doors that stand between us, their strong locks and my weakness, else your complaints would cease and I should be happy!

CALISTO. What's this, my lady? Do you expect me to allow a piece of wood to spoil our pleasure? I thought that nothing but your will could prevent it. Oh these damned, bothersome doors! I wish God would smite them with the hot fire that's burning me! With even the third part of it they'd be instantly consumed! In God's name, my mistress, let me have my servants break them down!

PARMENO. Didn't I tell you, Sempronio? He's going to get us into trouble! I don't like this visit at all. It's an unlucky business, I think. I'm leaving.

SEMPRONIO. Shut up and listen. She won't let him.

MELIBEA. Oh my dear, don't ruin me and hurt my good name! Control yourself. You'll not be disappointed. You have only to wait until we meet. Be satisfied with seeing me tomorrow night at this time in the garden. If you break down the doors, even though we weren't discovered, it would raise a terrible suspicion of me in my father's house and it would be noised about the city, for, as they say, the greater the one who errs, the greater the error.

SEMPRONIO. This is a bad night for us! Our master is so dilatory that we'll be caught by daylight. We've been here so long already that they've probably heard us in Melibea's house or next door, unless luck is with us.

PARMENO. I've been begging you to leave for the last two hours. We're in for it, sure!

CALISTO. Oh my mistress, my darling! How can it be an error if God's own saints have brought it about? I was praying at the altar of the Magdalene when our good woman brought me your message.

PARMENO. Rave on, Calisto, rave on! I verily believe, brother, that he's no Christian! How could he be when he says that what that old traitor contrived with her stinking spells was the work of God's saints? And he was going to break down the doors by their authority! At the first blow, Pleberio's servants, who are sleeping hard by, would have waked up and nabbed him!

SEMPRONIO. Don't let it worry you, Parmeno. We're quite a way off. As soon as we hear anything we'll run. Let him do what he likes. If he makes a mistake he'll pay for it.

PARMENO. You read my thoughts. Leave him be. Let's not get ourselves killed; we're too young. How you'd laugh to see me now, brother! I'm half turned, my legs are spread, my left foot's forward, my skirts are tucked under my belt, and my shield is rolled up under my arm so as not to get in the way. By God, I could run like a wild goat, I'm that scared!

SEMPRONIO. I've done even better. I've got my shield and sword tied together by their straps so I won't drop them when I run, and I've got my helmet in my hood.

PARMENO. What did you do with the stones you had in it?

SEMPRONIO. I threw them out to lighten the load. I've got enough to carry with the breastplate you made me wear. I should have refused; it's too heavy for running. Listen! Did you hear that, Parmeno? Something's going on! It's all up with us! Set out for Celestina's house so they'll leave the way open to ours!

PARMENO. Run, you slowpoke! Damn me! If they gain on us throw away your shield and the rest.

SEMPRONIO. I wonder if they've killed our master yet.

PARMENO. I don't know. Don't talk. Run and keep your mouth shut! He's the least of my worries.

SEMPRONIO. Parmeno, come back! It was only the watch that was making that noise in the next street.

PARMENO. You'd better make sure. Don't trust your eyes. You often take one thing for another. They didn't leave a drop of blood in my body! I thought I was dead! I felt them sticking me in the back! I've never been so scared in my life! Or in such a pickle! And I've been in plenty of tight spots before this. I worked for the friars of Guadalupe for nine years and was in a thousand street fights, but this is the first time I thought I was going to die.

SEMPRONIO. Well, didn't I work for the priest of St. Michael's? But God help you if you wear armor! That's something really to put the fear of death in you! As they say, loaded with iron, loaded with fear! Come back, come back! It was only the watch.

MELIBEA. My lord Calisto, what's that noise in the street? It sounds like men running. Take care of yourself, for God's sake. You're in danger!

CALISTO. Don't be afraid, mistress; I'm well guarded. It must have been my lads, who are wild enough to disarm everyone they meet. They were chasing someone.

MELIBEA. Have you got many men?

CALISTO. Only two, but even if there had been six against them it wouldn't have bothered my lads to disarm them and put them to flight, they're so spirited. I picked them myself, my lady; I didn't hire them just for tonight. If they hadn't held back out of regard for your reputation, they'd have knocked these doors to pieces, and if we'd been discovered they'd have protected us against all your father's men.

MELIBEA. For goodness' sake don't let them do such a thing! But I'm very glad you've got such faithful men to guard you. The bread that such sturdy servants eat is well spent. Since nature gave them such spirit, if you love me, sir, treat them well and reward them fittingly, so they'll keep our secret.

PARMENO. Sir, come away quickly! A crowd of men are coming this way with torches and you'll be recognized. There's no place to hide here.

CALISTO. What an unlucky wretch I am, to have to leave you, my mistress! It's only fear for your honor that could make me move from here, not fear of death! May the angels guard you! I'll come to the garden tomorrow night, as you said.

PLEBERIO. Wife, are you asleep?

ALISA. No, my lord.

PLEBERIO. Do you hear a noise in our daughter's bedchamber?

ALISA. I do indeed! Melibea! Melibea!

PLEBERIO. She doesn't hear you. I'll call louder. Melibea, my daughter!

MELIBEA. Sir?

PLEBERIO. Who is walking about and making that noise there?

MELIBEA. It's Lucrecia, sir. I sent her for a pitcher of water; I was very thirsty.

PLEBERIO. Go back to sleep, daughter. I was afraid it might be something else.

LUCRECIA. They sleep lightly! They sounded frightened.

MELIBEA. No animal is so tame that it doesn't turn fierce when its young are threatened. What would they have done if they'd known I had gone out?

SCENE 3.   *Calisto's house. Calisto, Sempronio, Parmeno.*

CALISTO. Close the door, lads; and you, Parmeno, bring up a candle.

SEMPRONIO. You should rest and sleep, sir.

CALISTO. I will. I certainly need it! What do you think now, Parmeno, of the old woman you praised so ill? What a thing she has done! How could it have been done without her?

PARMENO. I didn't realize how sick you were, or how noble and worthy Melibea is, so there's some excuse for me. I know Celestina and her ways, and it was my duty to tell you; but now she's like another person, she's so changed.

CALISTO. What do you mean, changed?

PARMENO. She's so different from what she was that I shouldn't have believed it without seeing it. But it's as true as you live!

CALISTO. Did you two hear what I said to my mistress? What were you doing? Weren't you afraid?

SEMPRONIO. Afraid, sir? I assure you the whole world wouldn't have been enough to scare us! You needn't worry on that score. We waited for you with our swords drawn, ready for anything!

CALISTO. Didn't you sleep just a little bit?

SEMPRONIO. Sleep, sir? You must think your servants are sluggards! I didn't even sit down, by God, or put my feet together, but kept looking in all directions so that at the first alarm I could jump and run to your help! And this Parmeno, who you thought was serving you so unwillingly, why, he was as happy to see those torchbearers as a wolf is when he sniffs a flock of sheep! He was going to take their torches away from them, until he saw they were too many.

CALISTO. I'm not surprised. It's his nature to be foolhardy. If he hadn't done it on my account he'd have done it anyway, for that's the way these fellows are. They can't go against their own disposition. The fox sheds her coat, but she can't shed her nature. Indeed, I told my mistress Melibea what kind of chaps you are, and how safe I was with you to guard me. I'm obliged to you, my lads. Pray God to keep you healthy, for I'll reward you more fully later on. God rest you!

PARMENO. Where shall we go, Sempronio, to bed or to the kitchen for a bite to eat?

SEMPRONIO. You may go wherever you like, but before daybreak I'm going to Celestina's to get my share of the chain. She's an old whore, and I don't want to give her time to cook up some lie and cheat us out of our part.

PARMENO. You're right; I'd forgotten. Let's go together, and if she tries anything we'll give her a scare she won't like. There's no friendship where money's concerned.

SCENE 4. *Celestina's house. Celestina, Sempronio, Parmeno, Elicia.*

SEMPRONIO. Quiet now! She sleeps next this window. (Knocks.) Mistress Celestina! Open the door!

CELESTINA. Who's there?

SEMPRONIO. Open up! It's your boys.

CELESTINA. You crazy brats! Come in, come in! What do you mean by showing up here at this time of night? It's almost day! What have you two been up to? What happened? Did Calisto miss his chance, or has he still got it? Or what?

SEMPRONIO. Or what, mother! If it hadn't been for us, by this time he'd be looking for his last resting place! Why, his whole estate wouldn't be enough to pay us for what we did for him, that is, if what they say is true, that a man's life is the most valuable thing he has!

CELESTINA. Jesus! What kind of row were you two mixed up in? Tell me about it, for God's sake!

SEMPRONIO. It was so outrageous that it makes my blood boil only to think of it!

CELESTINA. Sit down and tell me about it.

PARMENO. You're asking too much. We're too tired and sore from what we've been through. You'd do better to get us some breakfast. It might calm us down a bit. I swear I was so furious that I didn't want to meet a man of peace. I'd have liked nothing better than to run into someone to take my rage out on! I couldn't take it out on those who started the row, they ran so fast!

CELESTINA. I'm hanged if you don't frighten me, you're so fierce! But you must be joking. Sempronio, you tell me what happened.

SEMPRONIO. By God, I'm half out of my wits with rage! It's too bad I can't talk to you as I would to a man! But I never use my strength against the weak. My breastplate, mistress, is all in pieces; my shield has lost its handle; my sword looks like a saw; my helmet's in my hood, all dented. I haven't got anything left to wear when my master needs me to escort him, and he's going to see his lady tonight in her garden. I can't buy everything new. I haven't got a penny to clink on my tombstone!

CELESTINA. Get your master to buy them for you, my son, since you used them in his service. You know he'll make them good at once. He's not one of the kind who say: you can live with me, but get someone else to support you. He's so generous he'll give you all you want and more.

SEMPRONIO. Ha! Parmeno's arms are also ruined. At this rate our master's estate will all be spent to buy us arms. How can you expect us to demand more of him than he willingly gives, which is considerable? I don't want it said of me: they give him an inch and he takes an ell! He has already given us a hundred pieces of gold and his chain. With three such gouges he won't even have any wax left in his ears! This affair of his would come too high. Let's be satisfied with what's reasonable and not lose it all because we're too greedy. As they say, he who embraces too much can't squeeze very hard.

CELESTINA. The ass is funny! By my old age, if it were only a matter of eating, I'd say we've all done pretty well! Are you out of your mind, Sempronio? What has your reward got to do with my wages? Or your wages with my gifts? Is it up to me to mend your armor? Or make good your mistakes? Sink me if you haven't taken me up on a little word I let slip the other day, to the effect that everything I had was yours, and that to the limit of my meager strength I'd never fail you, and that, if God gave me a good hand with your master, you'd not be the loser! Well, Sempronio, you must know that such offers and polite words carry no responsibility. All is not gold that glitters. If it were it would sell more cheaply. Tell me, Sempronio, didn't I guess what was in your mind? I'm old, but I can still read your thoughts. To tell the truth, my son, I'm sorrier than I can say, because I gave the chain to Elicia to play with when I came from your house, and now she can't remember what she did with it. We haven't slept a wink all night, we're so worried, not so much over the value of the chain, which isn't great, but over her carelessness and my bad luck. Some friends came in about that time and I'm afraid they nipped it. You know how it goes: now you see it, now you don't.

Well, my sons, I'll say to both of you that if your master gave me anything I'm going to keep it. I didn't ask you, Sempronio, for part of your brocaded doublet, nor do I want it. Let's all serve him and he'll reward us as he thinks we deserve. He gave me what he did because I twice risked my life for him. I've dented more armor in his service than you two, and spent more money. You should bear in mind, my sons, that I used my own money and knowledge, which I didn't get by idling, as Parmeno's mother (God rest her soul!) is my witness. I did my work and you did yours. What I do, I do because it's my trade and my profession; what you do, you do for your amusement. Your reward, therefore, should not be as great as mine. However, if the chain shows up I'll give each of you a pair of scarlet breeches, which are most becoming to young men. If it doesn't, you have my blessing and I'll say nothing about my loss. I love you both, for you wanted me to have this job rather than another. Be satisfied with this, or you'll do yourselves no good.

SEMPRONIO. This isn't the first time I've remarked how strong this vice of avarice is among the old. Liberal in youth, miserly in old age! The more you get, the more you want; you get poorer as you get greedier; nothing makes the miser poorer than money! My God, how poverty increases with abundance! Didn't this old hag say I'd have all the profit from this business if I wanted it? But that was when she thought it wouldn't amount to anything, and now that she sees how much there is in it, she wants to keep everything for herself, just to prove the truth of the proverb: of little, little; of much, nothing!

PARMENO. She'll either give us what she promised, or we'll take it away from her! I told you plenty of times what this old witch was like, but you wouldn't believe me.

CELESTINA. Don't take your spite out on me just because you're sore at yourselves or your master or your armor. I know what's at the bottom of this; I know what foot you're limping on. It's not because you need money, or even because you're greedy, but because you think I've got you so tied up with Elicia and Areusa that you can't look around for others. That's why you're making these threats about money and trying to scare me. Don't worry. She who got them for you can get you ten others, now that you're wiser and more deserving. Parmeno will bear me out. Tell him, Parmeno. Don't be bashful. Tell him what you did with Areusa that time she was sick.

SEMPRONIO. That's enough talk! Try that bone on another dog! Give us our share of what you got from Calisto, unless you want to get shown up for what you are. Peddle your fine words elsewhere, old woman!

CELESTINA. Who do you think I am, Sempronio? Did you by chance get me out of some whorehouse? Shut your mouth! Don't insult my gray hairs! I'm an old woman as God made me, no worse than the rest. I live honestly by my trade like any artisan. I don't bother those who don't bother me. Whoever wants anything from me comes to my house for it. God is my heart's witness whether I live well or ill. And don't think you can mistreat me in your rage. There's justice for everyone: all are equal before it. I'm only a woman, but they'll listen to me as readily as they will to you, with all your prettiness! Leave me alone in my house. And you, Parmeno, don't think you've got a hold on me just because you know my past and the misfortunes I shared with your unhappy mother in our good days.

PARMENO. Don't fill my nostrils with the stench of your reminiscences! If you don't stop it I'll send you packing to her where you'll have something to complain about!

CELESTINA. Elicia! Elicia! Get up out of that bed and fetch me my cloak! By God's saints I'll go to the authorities howling like a lunatic! What's this? Threatening me in my own house? You think you can bully a tame sheep? A tied hen? An old woman of seventy? Go pick a fight with men like yourselves, armed with swords, not distaffs!

SEMPRONIO. You old miser, with your throat parched for money! You won't be satisfied with the third part of our earnings?

CELESTINA. What third part? Get out of my house! And you, Parmeno, stop that shouting! Do you want to bring out the neighbors? Don't drive me mad! Don't air Calisto's affairs and yours!

SEMPRONIO. Scream your head off, but you're going to do what you promised, or this is your last day on earth!

ELICIA. Put away your sword, for God's sake! Hold him, Parmeno! Don't let that madman kill her!

CELESTINA. Help! Help! Neighbors! These ruffians are killing me!

SEMPRONIO. Ruffians, is it? Wait a bit, mistress witch, and I'll send you to hell with a proper passport!

CELESTINA. Oh! He's killing me! Oh! Oh! Confession!

PARMENO. Hit her! Hit her! Finish her off, now you've begun! What if they do hear us! Let her die! One enemy the less!

CELESTINA. Confession!

ELICIA. You wicked men! I hope you pay for this! Look what you've done! My mother and my comfort, dead!

SEMPRONIO. Run, Parmeno, run! A lot of people are coming! Look to yourself! Here comes the watch!

PARMENO. There's no place to go! They've blocked the door!

SEMPRONIO. Out the window! Don't let them get us!

PARMENO. Jump! I'll follow you!

ACT XIII

Calisto's house.   Calisto, Tristram, Sosia.

CALISTO. How well I slept after my sweet adventure, my heavenly discourse! How well I rested! Was it because I was happy? Did I sleep merely because I was tired, or because of the glorious exaltation of my spirit? Most likely all these things combined to padlock my eyes, for my body worked no less than my spirit last night. How true it is that sadness brings melancholy and that melancholy prevents sleep, as with me these past days when I doubted I'd ever attain my desire! Oh my mistress Melibea! My love! What are you thinking now? Are you thinking of me or of another? Are you asleep or awake? Are you still in bed? Oh happy and fortunate Calisto! Can this be true, or have you dreamed it? Could I have dreamed it? Was it a fantasy, or did it really happen? But I was not alone; my servants were with me, two of them. If they say it really happened I'll have to believe them. I'll have them called. Tristram! Boys! Tristram! Get up!

TRISTRAM. I'm up, sir.

CALISTO. Run and call Sempronio and Parmeno for me.

TRISTRAM. At once, sir.

CALISTO.

> *Sleep, thou troubled one, and rest,*
> *   And fear no more;*
> *Thy lovely mistress loves thee well*
> *   Whom all adore.*

Carking care is vanquished quite
By pleasure sheer,
For thou art Melibea's own
True lover dear.

TRISTRAM. Sir, there's no one here.

CALISTO. Open the shutters and see what time it is.

TRISTRAM. The day is well along, sir.

CALISTO. Well, close them again and let me sleep till dinner time.

TRISTRAM. I'll go down to the door and see that no one disturbs my master's sleep. . . . But what's all that shouting in the marketplace? What is it, I wonder? Either someone's getting hanged, or the people have got up early to run the bulls. But here is Sosia; he'll tell me what's going on. The rascal is all disheveled. He must have been rowing in some tavern. If my master sees him in that state he'll have him beaten to a pulp. He's a bit cracked, but a good beating will bring him round. He seems to be crying. What's the matter, Sosia? Why are you crying? Where have you been?

SOSIA. Woe is me! What a fearful loss! What a dishonor for my master's house! What an evil day! Oh the poor lads!

TRISTRAM. What's the matter with you? Why are you going on like that? What evil are you talking about?

SOSIA. Sempronio and Parmeno. . . .

TRISTRAM. What about Sempronio and Parmeno? What are you trying to say, fool? Explain yourself. Don't irritate me.

SOSIA. Our brothers, our brothers. . . .

TRISTRAM. You're either drunk or out of your wits, or you bring bad news. Are you going to tell me what this is about those lads?

SOSIA. They've been beheaded in the square!

TRISTRAM. If that's true it's terrible news for us! Let's go tell our master.

SOSIA. Sir!

CALISTO. What's this, fools? Didn't I tell you not to disturb me?

SOSIA. Wake up and dress, sir. If you don't protect us we're lost! Sempronio and Parmeno have been executed in the square as public malefactors, with the town crier proclaiming their crime!

CALISTO. God help me! What are you saying? I can't believe this sudden calamity. Did you see them?

SOSIA. I saw them.

CALISTO. Are you sure? Why, they were with me this very night!

SOSIA. Well, they got up early enough to lose their heads!

CALISTO. Oh my faithful servants! Oh my willing workers! Can this be true? Oh unfortunate Calisto! What will become of you now, with these two dead? In God's name, Sosia, tell me what they did! What did the crier say? Where were they arrested? What magistrate had them executed?

SOSIA. Sir, the headsman said: "Justice commands that murderers be put to death!"

CALISTO. Who was ever so promptly executed? What can be behind this? Why, they left me not four hours ago! Who was the victim?

SOSIA. A woman called Celestina.

CALISTO. What are you saying?

SOSIA. Just what you hear.

CALISTO. If that is true you may kill me; you have my permission! If Celestina, she of the scar, is dead, nothing worse can be imagined!

SOSIA. It was she. I saw her body lying in her house, stabbed more than thirty times. One of her servants was crying over it.

CALISTO. Poor boys! How did they take it? Did they see you? Did they speak to you?

SOSIA. Oh sir, it would have broken your heart to see them! One was senseless, with his brains running out, and the other had both his arms broken and his face smashed. They were covered with blood. They had jumped out of a high window to get away from the watch and were almost dead when they were beheaded. I don't think they felt anything.

CALISTO. But my honor! Would to God I were in their place and had lost my life but not my honor! And now I have no hope of carrying my plan to its purposed end, which is what I most regret in this disastrous event! How my good name will be bandied about from mouth to mouth! And how my most hidden secrets will be peddled in the squares and marketplaces! What will become of me? Where can I go? Why go to the square if I can no longer help the dead? Why stay here? It would look like cowardice. Who can advise me? Tell me, Sosia, why did they kill her?

SOSIA. Her servant, sir, the one who was screaming, was telling everyone that it was because she wouldn't share with them the gold chain you gave her.

CALISTO. What a fatal day! What a day of woe! How my goods are passed from hand to hand and my name from tongue to tongue! Everything will be made public, everything they knew of me, as well as the matter they were engaged in! I'll not dare show my face among men. Oh unlucky youths, to come to such a sudden and calamitous end! How my happiness is undone! It's an old saying, that the higher one climbs the greater will be his fall. Last night I climbed high; today I lost everything. Rare is a calm day upon the sea. I should have sailed serenely if my fate had quieted the winds of my destruction. Oh fortune, how you have proved to be my adversary on every hand! But, however my house is persecuted, and however I am persecuted, adversity must be met with unwavering courage, for thus the heart is proved weak or strong. There's no better touchstone by which a man proves the fineness of his metal. . . .

Well, whatever evil comes to me, I'll not fail to obey the command of her who was the cause of all this, for I've got more to gain by winning the glory I hoped for than in mourning those who died. They were insolent and arrogant and would have been brought to account sooner or later. The old woman was wicked and false, and they quarreled over the spoils. It was the will of providence that she should die for the many adulteries she was responsible for. I'll have Sosia and little Tristram escort me and bring a ladder, for the walls are very high. Tomorrow, if I can do nothing about avenging the deaths of the others, I'll pretend that I've been out of town. If I can't, my pretended absence will establish my innocence.

ACT XIV

Pleberio's garden. Melibea, Lucrecia,
Sosia, Tristram, Calisto.

MELIBEA. Our gentleman is very late. What do you think, Lucrecia?

LUCRECIA. He has been delayed, my lady, by something he cannot help.

MELIBEA. May the angels guard him and keep him from harm! I am not so much worried by his being late as by thinking of the many things that could happen to him between his house and mine. . . . But listen! I hear footsteps in the street, and I even think I hear talking beyond the garden wall.

SOSIA. Set the ladder, Tristram. It's pretty high here, but it's the best place.

TRISTRAM. Go up, sir. I'll go with you. We don't know who may be inside. I hear voices.

CALISTO. Quiet, fools! I'll go alone. It's my mistress.

MELIBEA. It is your slave, your captive! It is she who values your life above her own! Oh my lord, do not jump from such a height! I shall die watching you! Come down slowly. Don't be in such a hurry.

CALISTO. Oh my angel! My precious pearl! When I see you all the world looks ugly! I have you in my arms and I cannot believe it! I am so beside myself with joy that I cannot feel the joy I have!

MELIBEA. What is this, my lord? I give myself into your hands because I love you and you treat me as if I were your enemy? Would you destroy me for the sake of a moment's pleasure? Once a wrong is done it cannot be undone. Enjoy what I enjoy, the sight of the beloved. How can you demand of me what you cannot restore with all the treasure in the world?

CALISTO. Mistress, I have risked my life to win this favor. What sense would there be in rejecting it now? You cannot ask me to do so, nor could I so betray myself. No man could, if he were a man! Especially one who loves as I love! Long have I been swimming in this hot sea of desire. Would you refuse me sanctuary in your dear port, or rest from my hardships?

MELIBEA. Oh my life! Say what you will, but please keep your hands away! Restrain yourself, my lord!

CALISTO. Why, mistress? And leave my passion unfulfilled? And go back to my suffering and begin this game all over again? Forgive my shameless hands, my lady! In their unworthiness they never expected to touch even your garments, and now they exult in the touch of your lovely body and your beautiful and delicate flesh!

MELIBEA. Leave us, Lucrecia.

CALISTO. Why should she, my lady? I should be happy to have such a witness of my glory!

MELIBEA. But not I, to have a witness of my shame! Had I thought you would be so reckless I had not trusted myself to you!

SOSIA. Tristram, you can hear them. How are things going?

TRISTRAM. I've heard enough to judge my master to be the luckiest man ever born! By my life, even though I'm only a youngster, I could give as good an account of myself as he!

SOSIA. Anyone could, with such a jewel! But he has made his bed; let him lie in it. It will cost him dearly. Two servants have gone into the making of that sauce!

TRISTRAM. He has forgotten them. Go get yourself killed serving scoundrels and do mad deeds in their defense! . . . . How happy they are in their embraces, and their servants beheaded and disgraced!

MELIBEA. Oh my dear lord, how could you have despoiled me for such a brief pleasure? Oh my poor mother, if you knew of this you would gladly kill yourself or me! You would be the executioner of your own flesh and blood, and I the melancholy cause of your death! Oh my honored father, how I have besmirched your good name and brought low your house! Oh my faithless one, why did I not first think of the great evil that would come from seeing you, and the great danger in store for me?

SOSIA. *I'd like to be the one listening to those bewailings! They all recite the same litany after it's too late! And that fool Calisto taking it in!*

CALISTO. Is dawn breaking already? How can that be? It seems only an hour that I've been here and the clock is striking three!

MELIBEA. In God's name, my lord, since you now are all I have and I am your mistress and you cannot deny my love, do not fail to pass my door by day and let me see you! You may see me by night whenever you will! Go now with God, for it is still dark and you will not be seen; nor will they hear me in my house.

CALISTO. Set the ladder, lads.

SOSIA. It's ready, sir.

MELIBEA. Come to me, Lucrecia. I am alone. My lord has gone. He left his heart with me and took mine with him. Did you hear us?

LUCRECIA. No, mistress; I was asleep. . . . But listen! Something terrible has happened!

MELIBEA. What is it? What are you saying?

TRISTRAM. Oh my dear master! Dead? Poor fellow, crushed and unconfessed! Sosia, gather up our luckless master's brains from the stones and put them back into his skull. Oh fatal day! Oh sudden death!

MELIBEA. What is it? Alas! What bitter thing do I hear? Help me up the wall, Lucrecia, and let me see my sorrow, lest I bring down my father's house with my screams! My comfort and my happiness, all vanished? My joy all lost? My glory consumed?

LUCRECIA. Tristram, my dear, what are you saying? Why do you weep so disconsolately?

TRISTRAM. I'm weeping over my great misfortune, my many troubles. My master Calisto fell from the ladder and died. His head is crushed. He died unconfessed. Tell his bereaved mistress that she'll not see her lover again. Sosia, do you take his feet and together we'll bear away the body of our dead master, lest his honor suffer, even though he died in such a place. Let distress follow us and sadness be our company! Let mourning and sackcloth be our garb!

MELIBEA. Oh saddest of the sad! How tardy came my pleasure! How quickly my grief!

LUCRECIA. Don't mar your face, my mistress, or tear your hair! A moment ago so happy, now so sad! What evil planet so suddenly changed its course! Don't be faint-hearted! Get up, in God's name, or your father will find you in this suspicious place! You'll be discovered! Don't you hear me, my mistress? Please don't faint! Be as strong to suffer your grief as you were bold to take your pleasure.

MELIBEA. Don't you hear what those lads are saying? Don't you hear them mourning, chanting the responses for the dead as

they bear away my life, my dead happiness? I can live no longer!
Why did I not enjoy my love? How could I have so little prized
my glory? Oh ungrateful mortals! You never know your happiness until you have lost it!

LUCRECIA. Arouse yourself, my mistress! This disgrace of being
found in the garden will be greater than the pleasure you felt in
his company or your grief at his death. Come to your chamber
and I'll put you to bed. I'll call your father and pretend you're
suffering from some other trouble. This will be hard to conceal!

ACT XV

*Pleberio's house. Pleberio, Melibea,
Lucrecia.*

PLEBERIO. What is it, Lucrecia? Why such haste? What sudden mischief can it be that doesn't give me time to dress or even to get up?

LUCRECIA. Hurry, my lord, if you would see her alive! Her seizure is so violent that I don't know what it is, nor can I recognize her, she's so altered!

PLEBERIO. What is this, my daughter? What ails you? What is this strange malady? What are you so distraught? Look at me! It's your father! Speak to me! What brought on this sudden attack? What is it? What hurts you? What do you want? Speak to me! Look at me! Tell me what it is and it will be remedied. Don't send me to my grave with worry at the end of my days! You are all I have! Open your lovely eyes and look at me!

MELIBEA. Woe! Woe!

PLEBERIO. What woe can be as great as mine is at your grief? Your mother fainted when she heard of your sickness. She was so upset she couldn't come to you. Courage! Open your heart! Be strong and come with me to your mother. Tell me, my dear, why are you grieving?

MELIBEA. There's no hope for me!

PLEBERIO. Daughter, my beloved, do not, in God's name, let

your suffering drive you to despair! Your despair argues a lack of courage. Tell me your trouble and it will be remedied forthwith. There's no lack of doctors and servants, or whatever may be necessary to restore your health: neither herbs nor magic stones nor charms, nor secret things from the bodies of animals. Don't vex me further or torment me, or drive me out of my senses, but tell me, what is the matter?

MELIBEA. I've got a fatal wound in my heart that stops my speech. It's not like other sicknesses. My heart will have to be removed to cure it, for it's hidden in a most secret part.

PLEBERIO. You're too young to suffer the troubles of age. Youth is the time of pleasure and joy, the enemy of sorrow. Get up and we'll go strolling on the riverbank. Seeing your mother will cheer you and relieve your pain. Bear in mind that there's nothing worse for sickness than to avoid pleasure.

MELIBEA. We'll go where you like. Let's go up to the roof of the tower, my lord, where I can see the ships, and there, perhaps, my pain will be lessened.

PLEBERIO. We'll go up and Lucrecia will go with us.

MELIBEA. If you please, dear father, have some stringed instrument brought up, so I may mitigate my grief with playing and singing.

PLEBERIO. That is good, my daughter. It shall be done at once. I'll see to it.

MELIBEA. How high we are, Lucrecia, my friend! I'm sorry my father left me. Do you go down and tell him to come to the foot of the tower. I've got something to say to him that I neglected to tell my mother. . . . I'm alone! I've planned my death well! How comforted I am to think that my beloved Calisto and I shall soon be united! I'll close the door so no one can prevent my death. I wouldn't have my departure delayed or the way cut off by which I'll shortly join him. Everything is as I wish it. I'll have time to tell my lord Pleberio the reason for my prepared death. I do great wrong to his gray hairs, a grievous offense to his old age. I bring him sorrow with my wrongdoing, but I can no longer prevent it. Thou, oh God, who art witness of my words, see Thou how little is my strength, and how my senses and my will are in thrall to my great love for my lost one, and how much stronger it is than my love for my living parents!

PLEBERIO. Why are you alone up there, daughter Melibea? What do you wish? Shall I come up?

MELIBEA. No, dear father. You would only prevent what I must say to you. I shall soon die. The hour draws near when I shall be at rest and your sorrow will begin; my comfort, your pain, my relief; the end of my loneliness and the beginning of your solitude. No need now, my honored father, for stringed instruments to assuage my grief, but only for bells to toll my death. Have courage to hear me out and I shall tell you the cause of my necessary and welcome death. And do not interrupt me with words and weeping, for you would only grieve the more not knowing why I take my life. Ask me nothing, answer me nothing, but only listen. When the heart is stopped with anguish the ears are closed to counsel and fruitful words are wasted.

Hear my last words, dear father. I hope you will accept them, for you will not blame me then for my wrongdoing. Harken to the mournful lamentations that fill the city: the clamor of the bells, the cries of the people, the thunder of the guns. I was the cause of it. Because of me the nobility of the city are clad in mourning. Because of me many servants today are without a master, the poor without succor, the proud needy without alms. Because of me the most perfect gentleman keeps company with the dead. I it was who took the life of that model of gentleness, gallantry, comely dress, speech, carriage, courtesy, and virtue. I it was who gave to the earth to enjoy forever the most noble body, the sweetest youth born in the world in our day. It must astonish you to hear of my unwonted crimes. Let me explain.

Some days ago, dear father, a gentleman whom you knew well, Calisto by name, fell in love with me. You knew his parents and his high lineage; his virtues and goodness were known to all.

Such was his suffering from his love and so little his opportunity to speak with me that he made his passion known to an astute and sage old woman called Celestina. She came to me in his behalf and persuaded me to reveal my secret love, and I showed her what I had kept hidden from even my own dear mother. She won my confidence and brought about the fulfillment of his desire and mine. He loved me and I returned his love, and he accomplished his ill-fated purpose. I admitted him to your house; he scaled the garden wall and broke through my defenses. And as he left, inconstant fortune disposed and ordained that, the wall being high, the night dark, and his servants unskilled in that kind of service, he should miss his footing, and he fell and dashed out his brains against the stones. The fates cut his thread; they cut off his life without confession; they cut off my hope, my glory, and my companion. Would it not be cruel, dear father, for me to live in pain, now that he is dead? His death invites mine; it beckons me to cast myself from a height in order to follow him. Let it not be said of me: the dead and the absent have no friends! Thus I shall give him the pleasure dead that I could not give him living.

Oh my love! My lord Calisto! Wait for me! I am coming! Stay just a little while. Do not chide me for my tardiness while I make this last accounting to my old father, for I owe him much.

Oh my dearly beloved father, I beseech you, as you loved me in this troublous life, to bury us together and let our funerals be together! I would offer you words of consolation before my longed-for death, words taken from the books you had me read to give light to my mind, save that my tortured memory and my grief have caused me to forget them, and the tears I see coursing down those wrinkled cheeks. Remember me to my beloved mother and tell her the sad reason of my death. How glad I am she is not here! Take refuge, dear father, in the solace of age, for long days give room for the enduring of long sadness. Receive now the meed of your reverend years; receive your beloved daughter! I am sad for myself, but sadder for you, and sadder still for my old mother. God be with you both! To Him I commend my spirit and to you my body!

ACT XVI

Pleberio's house. Pleberio, Alisa.

ALISA. What ails you, my lord Pleberio? Why those loud cries? I was beside myself today with grief when I heard of our daughter's seizure, but now your groans and shrieks, your tears and anguish, and your unwonted laments so disturb my heart, my very bowels, that my former pain is quite forgotten. Tell me why you weep and why you curse your honorable old age. Why do you plead for death to take you? Why do you tear those white hairs and wound that honored face? Is something amiss with Melibea? In God's name tell me, for if she is hurt I will no longer live!

PLEBERIO. Alas, noble wife! Our hope is gone and all our joy is lost! Let us now die! If you would share my grief and go quickly to your grave from sudden pain, look down and behold her whom I begot and you bore, now crushed and broken! She told me the reason of it and her sorrowing maid told me more. Help me to mourn our sad last days! Oh my people, witness my grief! Oh gentle friends, help me to bear my anguish! Oh my daughter, my delight! How can I bear to live, now that you are dead? How much more fitting had it been for the grave to take my three score years and ten and spare your scant twenty! This sad event has changed death's order.

Why did I grow old and gray, only to suffer? Happier would the earth have been to receive these white hairs than the golden ones I see before me! I have too long to live! Why should I not welcome death and complain of its delay? Must I be alone all this long while without you, my daughter? Let my life end here, now that you are gone! Oh my dear wife, if you still live arise and spend your last days with me in groans and broken sighs; but if by chance you have already joined her and left me to this troubled life, why did you leave me to bear it alone? Women have the advantage of us in this, that they can die of grief, and quickly, or at least lose their senses, which is a kind of comfort. Oh this too enduring father's heart! Why does it not break with grief, now that my beloved child is gone? For whom did I build towers? For whom did I plant orchards? For whom did I build ships? How can the pitiless earth sustain me? Where will my disconsolate age find refuge? Why did inconstant fortune, dispenser and stewardess of worldly goods, not vent her wrath, her changing moods, upon what is subject to her? Why did she not destroy my patrimony, or burn my house, or devastate my lands? If she had spared that plant in bloom and given me a happy old age after a troubled youth, she would not have perverted her natural order. I could better have suffered her deceits and persecutions in the time of my strength than in my last weak days.

Oh life, full of troubles and misery! Oh world, world! Many have written of its practices and compared it with many things, but they spoke from hearsay. I will describe the world as one who has been cheated in its false marketplaces. Thus far I have held my peace, lest the world in anger wither before her time the flower it took from me today. But now, like the penniless traveler who goes his way singing, without fear of the cruel highwayman, so goes my daughter, free of the world's vexatious company.

When I was young I thought the world was ruled by order. I know better now! It is a labyrinth of errors, a frightful desert, a den of wild beasts, a game in which men run in circles, a lake of mud, a thorny thicket, a dense forest, a stony field, a meadow full of serpents, a river of tears, a sea of miseries, effort without profit, a flowering but barren orchard, a running spring of cares, a sweet poison, a vain hope, a false joy, and a true pain. The world sets its traps for us baited with delights, and when we most enjoy them, then is the hidden hook discovered from which we may not free ourselves, for our wills are held captive. The world puts us away from it lest we call it to account for its deceitful promises. Carefree and at breakneck speed we course the field of its abundant vices, only to fall at last into the pit from which we cannot escape. Many have left the world for fear the world would abandon them. Such may well call themselves blessed when they see the reward this sad old man has got for his long service. The world blinds us and then anoints our eyes with consolations. It spares none so that none will be alone in his affliction, for misery, it says, loves company! Oh woebegone old man, how alone am I!

I am struck down with no companion to share my grief. Had I the austere fortitude of that Paulus Aemilius who, having lost his two sons in seven days, had the spirit to console himself by consoling the Roman people, still I should not be satisfied, for he had the two adopted sons they gave him. And how can Pericles share my grief, that captain of Athens, or the valorous Xenophon, whose sons were lost while absent in foreign lands? It was not difficult for the one to show a serene countenance, or for the other to tell the messenger who brought the sad news not to grieve, since himself felt no regret. How different is theirs from my affliction!

Even less can this world of troubles say that Anaxagoras and I are alike in our loss, or tell me to answer with him, when he lost his only son and I my beloved daughter: "I am mortal and whom I beget must die!" Because my Melibea killed herself by her own hand and before my eyes, from the great grief and torture of her love, while he was killed in lawful battle. Oh incomparable loss! Oh stricken old man! The more I seek comfort the less reason do I find for comfort. The prophet David, who mourned when his son fell sick, refused to mourn his death, saying it was folly to lament the irrecoverable, for he had many left with whom to heal his wound. Woe is me! I mourn her death less than the dreadful occasion of it. No longer shall I know, my luckless daughter, the fears and startings that daily used to frighten me, for your death has made fear meaningless.

What shall I do when I go into your chamber and find it empty? What shall I do when I call and you answer me not? Who can fill this great void you have left in me? Who has ever lost what I have lost today? Not even the great-hearted Lambas of Auria, Duke of Genoa, who took his son in his arms and cast him into the sea. For such are deaths that occur in the cause of honor. But what made my daughter slay herself but the strong force of love? So what comfort can the false world offer me for my weary old age? How can it expect me longer to stay here, knowing as I do its frauds, its snares, its chains and its nets, with which it captures our weak wills? Where will my daughter be? Who will dwell with me in my lonely house? Who will care for me in my halting years?

Oh love, love! How little did I think it strong enough to kill its subjects! In my youth it wounded me and burned me with its fires. Did it free me then only to collect its debt in my old age? When I had reached the age of forty and was happy with my dear companion, and then when I saw the blessed fruit of our union, today, alas!, cut off, I thought I was free of love. I little thought that it would visit upon the children its spite against the parents. Love causes men to prize the ugly and the ugly to seem beautiful to them. Who gave love such might? Who gave it that name so little fitting? For if love were love indeed it would not afflict its servants, and if they lived happily they would not slay themselves, as did my beloved daughter!

How love serves its ministers! The false procuress Celestina died at the hands of the faithfullest companions she ever had in her poisonous service. They died beheaded, Calisto died cast from a height, and my poor daughter chose the same death. Love has a sweet name, but what bitter deeds it does! Love distributes its gifts unequally, but that law which treats not all alike is an iniquitous law. We rejoice at the sound of love's name, but are made sad by too much traffic with it. Blessed are those who know not love, and those whom love passes by! Some have called love a god, induced thereto by some error of the senses; but God nourishes whom He kills, while love slays its followers. Love is the enemy of all reason and gives its gifts to those who serve it least, until they too are caught in love's mournful dance. Love is an enemy of friends and a friend of enemies, and knows no order in its rule. Love is painted blind, poor, and young, and is given a bow with which it shoots at random; but blinder are love's ministers who do not see how bitter will be their wages!

Love's burning ray leaves no mark where it strikes. Its fire is fed by the souls and lives of countless human creatures, not only Christians, but gentiles and Jews, which is their reward for their service. Consider Macias, he of our own day, who died of love and whose death was caused by love. Consider what Paris did for love, and Helen, and Hypermnestra, and Aegisthus! All the world knows! And Sappho, Ariadne, Leander, how were they rewarded? And David and Solomon, were they spared? And did not Samson get his just deserts because of love, believing her whom love caused him to believe? Many others there are whom I shall not name, for I would speak of my own tribulations.

I accuse the world because it gave me life, for had it not done so, I had not begotten Melibea; had she not been born, she had not loved; and had she not loved, these troubled and disconsolate last days of mine had never been!

Oh my good companion, my broken daughter! Why did you not allow me to save you? Why had you no pity for your well loved mother? Why such cruelty for your aged father? Why did you forsake me, knowing I had to leave you soon? Why did you afflict me and leave me sad and alone in this vale of tears?